T5-DHH-331

enchanted ❤ 5 HEARTS

Spellbound

Phyllis Karas

AN AVON FLARE BOOK

This is a work of fiction. Names, characters, places, and incidents either
are the product of the author's imagination or are used fictitiously. Any
resemblance to actual events, locales, organizations, or persons, living or
dead, is entirely coincidental and beyond the intent of either the author or
the publisher.

AVON BOOKS, INC.
1350 Avenue of the Americas
New York, New York 10019

Copyright © 1999 by Phyllis Karas
Excerpt from *Love Him Forever* copyright © 1999 by Cherie Bennett and
Jeff Gottesfeld
Published by arrangement with the author
Library of Congress Catalog Card Number: 99-94732
ISBN: 0-380-78990-6
www.avonbooks.com

First Avon Flare Printing: October 1999

AVON FLARE TRADEMARK REG. U.S. PAT. OFF. AND IN OTHER COUNTRIES, MARCA
REGISTRADA, HECHO EN U.S.A.

Printed in the U.S.A.

WCD   10   9   8   7   6   5   4   3   2   1

Spellbound

𝓜y mother is a witch. My brother is a warlock. My father owns a hardware store. And I'm a 15-year-old, relatively decent soccer player who owes her new-found athletic ability to an unexpected exhibition of supernatural powers. Okay, so we're not your typical American family, but this family is the only one I've got, and besides, there's not a darn thing I can do about it. But perhaps I should explain . . . it hasn't always been this way.

Just six short months ago, my mother was a feature reporter for our hometown newspaper and my brother was an underachieving high school senior who also happened to be the best-looking guy and the biggest troublemaker in his class. My father already owned the hardware store, but I couldn't run two inches with a soccer ball without falling headfirst into the grass. How did we change from a slightly dysfunctional family to the Addams Family? It was simple. We met Sarah Goody.

Or rather, my mom met Sarah Goody. I remember the day so clearly it scares me, because I'm famous for not remembering anything, especially class assignments, dentist appointments, and where I left more than three-fourths of my wardrobe.

But that day will never fade from my mind. I remember it was a Monday, because I stayed after for the soccer game against Peabody. It was my typical soccer game. I sat on the bench until the last minute, when we were up by five goals and our coach, Avis Goldstein, decided to let me and Pam Brown, the other loser on our team, onto the field. I stood there, frozen as always, hating the soccer ball even more than I hated the coach. Why I was on the team in the first place was a mystery to anyone who saw me play. It was some weird combination of having a crush on Brian Walsh, who was on the boys' soccer team; being best friends with Carrie Burns, the captain and best player on the freshman girls' soccer team; and having a mother who couldn't handle the fact that her only daughter was a klutz. Of course, I fully understood that my mother's three-part series on the girls' sports program at Rockmere High School was the major reason I was wearing a girls' soccer uniform.

Anyhow, I failed to block a shot, and we ended up winning by only four goals, but no one cared. The game was over, I was terrible, and Carrie was a star. We walked home together, and she gave me her usual pep talk, effortlessly kicking a ball in front of us. I ignored her and gave all my attention to Brian Walsh, who suddenly had appeared next to me. I wanted to say something cool like "Hi, Brian," but instead, I tripped over the ball. Brian laughed and helped me up and said something, but I couldn't hear it because I had died inside and was just waiting for the rest of me to catch up. "You going to help us decorate for the dance?" Carrie asked Brian while I prayed that if I tripped again, this time I would simply fall into a manhole and never be seen again.

"Sure," Brian answered her. "That dance sounds like it's gonna be great."

Oh, God, I moaned to myself, *don't let him ask her right here in front of me. Spare me that agony. Please.*

"It sure is," Carrie said. "I hope everyone comes."

"Who'd want to miss it?" Brian asked, and I started to pray silently again, this time for a manhole to swallow me up. As I stared at the ground, I could feel Brian looking at me. I looked up at him and he quickly glanced away.

A few seconds later, Brian left me and Carrie at the corner of my street, saying "See you." I knew, like I knew the world was round, that his "See you" had been directed at Carrie, but the same part of my brain that forced me onto the soccer field refused to accept that fact. Carrie was not only the best soccer player on our team, she was a gorgeous knockout. I should have hated her for being so perfect, but instead I loved her. She'd been my dearest, most trusted friend since she moved to Rockmere in second grade and sat next to me in Mrs. Ellison's class.

I was still replaying Brian's words in my head when Carrie and I walked into my kitchen. We had just whipped ourselves up a couple of sundaes when my mom came in. She was carrying her briefcase and a bag of groceries, and was wearing her favorite suit, a red pleated skirt and matching red-and-blue jacket. She always wears it when she goes on a new interview. Mom has long black curly hair and dark brown eyes and looks great in red. "Wow!" she said as she threw her briefcase and grocery bag onto the kitchen counter and sank into a chair beside me at the table.

Carrie and I looked at each other and shook our heads. Nobody was as concerned about what I eat as my mom, and the fact that she hadn't gone ballistic over my overflowing dish of ice cream, hot fudge, whipped cream, and Heath Bar chunks was ominous. I couldn't believe it, but I was not enjoying my sundae. I threw down my spoon. "What's going on, Mom?" I asked. "Are you on something or what?"

"I'm on something, all right," my mother answered, noticing my sundae for the first time. She shot me a disgusted look and pulled the dish away. I sighed with relief. She was back on the mother ship. "Just about the most interesting story I've ever worked on."

"Really?" Carrie asked, spooning more ice cream into her mouth as she talked. My mother could care less what Carrie ate. Perhaps the fact that Carrie and I are the same height but Carrie weighs 110 pounds and I tip the scale at 125 might explain her sentiments. "Is it more interesting than the popcorn vendor who wore his winter coat twelve months of the year? Or the kid who blew his finger off with the firecracker? Or the people who trap dogs with those horrible leghold traps? What's happening, Mrs. S.?"

"What's happening," my mother answered, her hand firmly locked on my ice cream dish, "is Sarah Goody, the Salem witch. You've heard of her, haven't you?" Carrie and I both shook our heads. "Oh, that's strange. I thought everybody had. Well, truthfully, I hadn't heard of her myself until Alan Lupo asked me to do a piece on her for Halloween. I've never had such an incredible interview. The woman is uncanny. She read my tarot cards and you simply will not believe what she told me. She knew everything there was to know about me. She knew I had a son and a daughter. That my son is adopted and gorgeous and trouble, and my daughter is not adopted and is chunky and good-natured." Chunky and good-natured. Yup,

4

that was me. I could feel the tears well up in my eyes.

"Now, Emily," my mother continued, "don't go getting your nose out of joint. You're far more than just chunky and good-natured, but you have to admit it wasn't a bad beginning. Especially the part about Simon being adopted."

I didn't have to admit anything. I bit back my tears. "Go ahead, Mom," I said, perhaps a bit too sarcastically. "She *really* sounds unbelievable. How on earth could any other human being besides you and me and Carrie know two such important facts about our family?"

"That was just the tip of the iceberg," my mother continued. "She knew I have two younger sisters, that one is divorced and the other is an unmarried doctor. She knew I had a biopsy on my right breast last year and that it was benign. She knew that Daddy is a great golfer and is tall and handsome and owns a hardware store. She knew Simon had his tonsils out on his third birthday. She knew that Nana has bad arthritis and a new condo in Florida. Now what do you think?"

"Wow!" Carrie said, now ignoring the melting ice cream and gooey hot fudge in her bowl. "Unbelievable. Did she know anything about me?"

"I didn't ask her," my mother admitted. "But I promise I will when I see her tomorrow."

"You're going back to her house tomorrow?" I asked. My mother prided herself on meeting the subjects of her articles only once. She always insisted that after she interviewed someone, she could get more information over the telephone more easily than she could by facing the person a second time. "Why?"

"Because tomorrow Sarah is going to do my past incarnations," she explained. "She'll find out exactly who I was in my past lives. I can hardly wait."

"I bet you were Cleopatra," Carrie said. "I mean, your hair is so curly now, but I bet you anything you once had straight black hair and long thick bangs."

My mother stared at Carrie thoughtfully for a minute. "You know, you might be right," she said. "When I saw the movie with Liz Taylor and Richard Burton, I couldn't sleep for days afterwards. I'm dying to go to Egypt, but Jerry always refuses. He says it's too dirty and hot. But I know it's not that way. Now, how would I know that if I hadn't already lived there?"

"From that book you read last summer," I reminded her. "The one you made me read. *Palace Walk*. It made Egypt seem anything but just hot and dirty."

"I suppose so," my mother admitted. "But I had special feelings about Egypt before I read that book. I'm sure that's why I read it in the first place. And that's just one life. I know I've had many others which weren't anywhere near as exciting. I just can't wait to find out what they were."

"Can I come?" Carrie asked. "You could pretend I was the photographer from the *Item*. I'm terrific with a camera."

I couldn't believe Carrie. She was acting as sick as my mother. I was the only one in the room who still had her head on straight. If anyone was going to take pictures of this crazy lady, it was me. "I'm the one taking photography this semester," I reminded them. "I'm doing terrific things with black-and-white shots, in case you guys forgot."

"I'm sure you are, Emmy," my mother said. "But the *Item* already assigned a photographer to take the photos for the interview. I told Sarah about your school Halloween dance, and she said she hopes no

6

one dresses up like an ugly old witch with a long warty ugly nose and a black broom. She says that's demeaning to real witches. Neither one of you was thinking of going as a witch, were you?"

"No," Carrie answered. "We'd never do that. But how 'bout we go as a hot dog and a roll?" That girl is so creative it's sickening. "I can wear my pink body suit and we can make you a yellow-and-brown robe so you'll look like a hot dog roll with mustard. We'll look so funny. Everyone will notice us."

"I can think of a few things I'd rather be than a roll," I said. "But if you include onions and relish, I might do it."

"If you were going, what costume would you wear, Mrs. S.?" Carrie asked my mother, who was staring intently at the palm of her hand.

"Oh, me?" she answered distractedly. "I don't know. I'd think of something."

"Come on, Mom," I said, shocked that for once I had beaten Carrie to the punch. "Get the black mop and bikini top ready. Cleopatra lives again."

My mother pulled her eyes away from her hand and forced a smile. "Great idea," she said with about as much enthusiasm as I had shown at my soccer game. Then she grabbed my hand and ran her finger across my palm. "Whew." She whistled. "You look just fine. But I have to warn you, honey. Treat me nice." She pointed to a line that ran across the center of her palm. "I had a feeling something was bothering Sarah when she read my palm. Now I see it. I'm not here for long."

I didn't know whether to laugh or cry, but there wasn't much time for me to make a choice. Before I could decide, the main threat to my mother's longevity stormed into the kitchen. "Hi, Simon," my mother

7

said, placing her hands back on the table.

My brother looked, as always, as good as a guy could look. He was wearing Levi's and a blue-and-white pinstriped shirt under a gray crewneck sweater. The look was pure Gap and perfect for him. His black hair was thick and shiny and fell appealingly over his eyes. Thick lashes that I would have given up at least two teeth to own framed the green eyes for which I would have surrendered another three teeth.

But even more than his great looks, it was the way Simon moved that affected every girl, except me, who saw him. He was tall and muscular, but he still had a lanky look to him that added something cute and approachable to his appeal. However, that cuteness ended the minute he entered our house. The glance he offered my mother and me was anything but appealing. Four or five years ago, it might have still been cute, but since he'd turned thirteen, my brother had developed an edge of nastiness that erupted like a blinding red light whenever he felt the need to annoy someone. And that someone was quite frequently a teacher or policeman. For the members of his family, he felt little need to annoy but rather a strong and continual urge to hurt.

The scenes with the teachers always hurt my parents deeply. Either Simon would get caught trying to pass off a phony note from my mother excusing his absence for the previous three days, or he would insult a teacher to her face, or he would fall asleep right under her nose. There were constant conferences with the teachers, the principal, and the guidance counselors, and everyone always confirmed that Simon was bright and far more capable than his work or behavior showed. Occasionally, he was suspended for a few days, but usually the teachers settled for no more punishment than detention. But for my parents, the embarrassment of having to face disgruntled teachers lasted longer than any detention Simon sat through. The scenes at home, with my parents unsuccessfully trying to control their anger and Simon sitting there with that "I couldn't care less" look on his face, were my detention.

The police incidents were more serious. It seemed a miracle that with his arrests for possession of alcohol, shoplifting, and destruction of public property (he'd removed the sign for Simon Road so many times the town stopped replacing it), Simon still didn't have a permanent record. Most of the policemen were always ready to haul him in, but one policewoman, Susan Mullen, liked him and kept telling my parents he would straighten out one day soon. My father was convinced Officer Mullen was the reason my brother wasn't in jail.

There were lots of people like Officer Mullen in my brother's life. Carrie was one. She got that pathetic look in her eyes every time she saw my brother. As for me, that same sight made me want to run as far away as I could. Sarah Goody might have some mystical powers, but it would take an entire coven of witches to figure out what to do with my big brother.

two
2

$\mathcal{D}$inner that evening was a typical meal at the Silver household. Five minutes were devoted to my pathetic soccer game, seven to my mother's interview, ten to my father's new shipment of lawn mowers, and every other second to Simon.

For the past five years, my brother has been a thorn in my family's side. He was far from perfect before then, but he's been out of control ever since he hit adolescence. In all fairness, I don't think Simon wants this role. The army of shrinks my parents have taken him to since his thirteenth birthday have all said that he acts the way he does because he has low self-esteem, probably related to the fact that he's adopted and I'm not. They said that Simon ignored these feelings for most of his childhood but it suddenly became too much for him to handle. I've never been particularly comfortable with that theory, because it makes me feel as if I'm the cause of Simon's problems, like it's my fault he's adopted and I'm not. One shrink said my parents are not strict enough with Simon and that's why he's always in trouble. Still another said his problems are related to his good looks and the way people react to them. And my favorite said that if an entire ship is sinking because of one poor sailor, it is better to discard him and let the others survive than lose the whole crew. My mother practically killed that doctor, even though I think he had a lot of smarts.

But every shrink has agreed that Simon's stunts have been downright scary. Like the time he borrowed my dad's new Camry without permission and backed out of the garage without opening the garage door. Or the time he got arrested for possession of alcohol on the way to the junior prom. Or the time he fell forty feet off the bleachers during a football game and landed, miraculously, on his butt, breaking only his sunglasses and his right wrist. Some have even been sort of funny, like the April Fool's phone call he made to his math teacher, informing him that three skunks had been spotted in his front yard and he'd better stay put till further notice. The poor guy never made it to school that morning to give the test he'd scheduled for Simon's class.

The list of Simon's escapades is too huge to relate, but every time he does something bad, we all suffer. My parents suffer because they always believe Simon has learned from his mistakes. And I suffer because I know he will never learn from any mistake and I will have to watch my parents suffer, over and over again.

My favorite shrink told me I had a terrible burden, having to be good to keep my parents sane. He was right. Whenever I'm in a situation where I might do something bad, like cheat on a history test or smoke on school grounds, I panic. The wounds Simon inflicts on my parents are often huge, but eventually they heal. If I misbehaved, it might kill them.

The amazing thing is that all my friends think I am the luckiest person in the world to be Simon's sister. "He's so gorgeous," Julie Smith is always telling me.

"Please let me come for supper one night so I can see him eat." That sure would be a lot of fun. Julie would not only get to see Simon eat, but if she was really lucky, she would also see him swear at my parents and hurl his plate of spaghetti against the wall.

"I would pay any amount of money for the chance to sleep at your house," Lindsay Margassian informed me the previous weekend. "Please, please, have a sleepover so I can sneak in and see Simon sleeping. I'll bring all the food and drinks, I promise." Lindsay's slept over at my house, but always on nights when Simon is definitely not coming home. I would never risk having my friends see Simon come in stinking drunk and create a huge scene with my parents.

Carrie used to be the only friend I had who understood what I go through with my brother. Still, it's hard because Simon is always sickeningly nice to her. And when he's nice to someone, that person is his for life. I know Carrie's developing a major league crush on him. "Of course, I believe you," Carrie says these days when I carry on about him. "It's just that I've never seen it firsthand." Once I called her during an especially hideous scene between Simon and my parents, but as soon as she answered the phone, Simon stopped the scene. "Maybe, just maybe, you're imagining some of it," Carrie once said to me. The look I gave her must have convinced her otherwise. I've tried to explain that he's only nice to her to aggravate me, but she doesn't listen.

That night at dinner, however, Simon was in rare form. The discussion subject was one of my all-time favorites: Simon's college plans. As a senior, he was supposed to be filling out college applications and getting high grades. Instead, he was cutting classes, flunking exams, and ignoring the pile of college applications my mother had placed on his desk. His SATs, of course, had been in the ninetieth percentile, just like his IQ. My brother wasn't stupid. Just rotten.

"I've found the perfect school for Simon," my mother announced before I'd had a chance to swallow my first piece of Shake 'n Bake chicken. "Hampshire College in Amherst. It's a nontraditional college, very interested in a student's potential, not just his accomplishments. They're totally unstructured and allow you to plan your own curriculum. Plus, it's part of the Amherst–Smith–Mount Holyoke–University of Massachusetts consortium. You can take classes at any of the four other colleges. What do you think, Simon?"

Simon was concentrating heavily on his chicken. One thing my brother does brilliantly is eat. He waited until he had an entire mouth full of chicken, mashed potatoes, and green beans before he answered, "Fabulouso!"

My mother smiled broadly. Even my father allowed himself a tiny movement of his lips. "I'm so glad you feel that way," my mother continued, more inspired by this one word than she'd been by Sarah Goody's entire tarot card reading. "Because I arranged an interview for you next Friday. While we're there, we might as well see Amherst and UMass, too, don't you agree, honey?"

Simon continued to eat, staring at his plate as if it were the most beautiful creature he'd ever seen. And my mother continued to rejoice in his incredible turnaround. I could see her mind working. Simon was out of our house, on a college campus, earning great grades, dating lovely coeds, developing into the brilliant young man she'd always known he could become. "Now, your boards will probably get you right in, but in case they don't, you'll have to work on your grades. I know you're having a bit of a problem with Mrs. Leventhal in math and Mr. Johnson in English. But we can get you a great math tutor, and I can help you write that paper on Willy Loman. What's important is that you attend your classes and keep a low profile."

"What's the tuition?" my father asked. "I'm sure it's a lot more than a state school."

My mother shot him a scathing look. "Don't worry, Jerry," she said. "I've been putting money aside for years. Wherever Simon wants to go, he will go. Emily, too."

"We've discussed this before, Ellen," my father said. You had to give the guy credit. My mother's evil look had little effect on him. He was tough. "We're going to have a hard time coming up with a hundred thousand dollars for the kids' college educations. This college sounds great, but it might be out of our ballpark."

I looked at my brother. He'd refilled his plate and was totally devoted to the food. "We'll figure something out," my mother informed my father. "The most important thing is that Simon find a college where he can prosper and develop intellectually." She was staring at Simon now. So was I. "So, you're finally getting a little excited about this whole college thing, huh?"

There was a sickeningly long silence while Simon stuffed his face. The guy was 6'2" and had a great physique, which was amazing since he never worked out and played no sports at all. But, man, could he eat. Unlike me, my brother never gained an ounce. Simon finally pushed his empty plate away, sat straight up in his chair, and let loose a disgusting burp. Then he wiped the gravy and butter off his chin with the back of his hand and burped a second time. "Fabulouso!" he repeated, only this time my mother understood his meaning: "Fabulouso meal."

My mother looked like she always did when Simon disappointed her: ready to cry but unable to shed a tear. "Okay," my father said slowly. "Okay, Simon. We get the message. The food was great but you're not biting on the college hook. Why don't you put your plate in the sink and let me enjoy the rest of my meal in peace?"

You have to feel bad for my father. The guy works hard, running his hardware store, finding things for his customers, and making sure his aisles are well stocked. Yet he comes home to a dinner hour that inevitably ends in unpleasantness. Sometimes it's just a minor skirmish, which is how I would categorize that evening's discussion. But most nights it's full-scale war, with weapons being fired and the two of us ducking for safety while Mom and Simon empty their guns into each other's bodies.

"No problemo," Simon said, picking up his plate and licking off its last tiny remnants with his long, curling tongue. "Like I said, 'Fabulouso.' " Without even glancing at my mother, whose eyes were riveted on him, my brother deposited his plate in the sink, scooped up a handful of Oreos, and departed the kitchen.

As always, the task of retrieving the bodies belonged to the surviving daughter. What I wanted to do was to put my dish in the sink, shove some cookies into my pocket, and book out of the kitchen just as Simon had done. But someone had to put Band-Aids on the wounds, or our parents would bleed to death.

"So, did you tell Dad about Sarah?" I asked my mother, who was still staring at the chair Simon had vacated. "I'm dying to hear what she had to say about him."

"Oh, yeah," my father said. He was always the first to come back to life, and he would help me bring Mom back, too. "I forgot about your interview with the witch. How did it go?"

"She said you were tall and thin and had slightly receding reddish hair," my mother said, looking at him now. Things were going well with her recovery. "She also said someone in our family was going to die earlier than expected." She grabbed my father's hand and ran her finger along his palm. "But don't worry. It's me."

"What are you talking about?" my father asked, pulling his hand away from hers. "Your mother is eighty and looks sixty. Both my parents died before they reached fifty. If anyone's going to die early in this family, it's me."

"Don't be ridiculous," my mother insisted. "It's me. Sarah just about said as much. But, truthfully, it's okay. I just know I've had incredible past lives, and I'm anxiously awaiting my next one."

I looked at my mother carefully. She had changed from her terrific red-and-navy suit to jeans and a Duke sweatshirt. I knew she was forty-three, but she usually looked much younger. Fights with my brother made her look weary and pained, and that night she looked every day of forty-three, maybe even fifty-three. Considering the slightness of the skirmish, I was surprised at her physical reaction. "Well, you're wrong," I told her. "It's not you. It's me."

"You?" my parents chorused.

"Yes, me," I said. "I've been having terrible pains

16

in my legs and chest. There is definitely something bad growing in my brain. And I can barely breathe when I walk onto the soccer field. I haven't wanted to worry you, but I'm on my way out of here."

"Emily, whatever are you talking about?" my father asked. One thing I will say about my dad is that he likes me a lot. My mother likes me, but she is so filled with Simon that she barely notices me unless I'm eating something incredibly unhealthy. But my father is in tune with my thoughts. If I were to check out, he would miss me a lot. "Since when haven't you been feeling good?"

"Since a long time," I said, actually beginning to feel dizzy. "But I don't want either of you to worry. It's probably going to be a long, drawn-out illness, so I'll be around for a while."

My mother shook her head and sighed loudly. "You saw *Love Story* again last night, didn't you?" she asked me.

I am too perfect to lie. "Yeah," I admitted. "I can't see how come Ali McGraw and Ryan O'Neal ended up has-beens. They were so fantastic in that movie. I'd do anything to have hair like hers."

"So, do I have to start paying your college tuition in three years?" my father asked, smiling now.

"I wouldn't pay for more than one year at a time," I told him. "Because I still think I might be under some sort of a bad spell."

"No problem," my mother said. "You'll come with me to Sarah's tomorrow when I finish my interview. I'll get her to check you out. You want to come too, Jerry?"

"Only if she can tell me how to turn a frog into a prince," he said, "without having to kiss him."

"I'll see if I can do it for you," my mom answered.

"How about you, Emmy? You game to go with me tomorrow?"

"I don't think so," I said, no longer anxious to meet this woman who had decreed that one of us must die. "I was just joking about the brain tumor. I'm fine."

"Oh, no, you're not," my mother said, grabbing my hand and holding it tightly. Only this time she wasn't looking at the lines that ran through my palm. She was rubbing the index finger on my right hand. "Aha! I knew it was still here. This wart, my love, has to go. And *you* are in luck. It's the full moon. Sarah can take care of it in her kitchen a heck of a lot easier than Dr. Ellerin can. She told me exactly how she does it. What about it? Liquid nitrogen or Sarah Goody? The choice is yours."

I was so glad to see both my parents smiling that I knew I had to go with Mom. I wasn't dying to meet this witch, never mind have her remove my wart, but what choice did I have? I was all these two had. Their wish—or should I say witch?—was my command.

three
ℒ

The next morning, my mother had her usual joyous time getting my brother out of bed. She knocked on his door a few minutes before seven, her voice upbeat and hopeful. "Are you up, honey?" she called out. There was never an immediate response, but my mother acted as if he had heard her. My father and I knew better. Simon's head was underneath his pillows, his alarm had not been set, and he had no intention of getting to school on time. For the next half hour, the same routine ensued: Every three minutes, my mother knocked and called out, her voice getting louder and more urgent with each knock. Finally, she would end up in the room, beside his bed, shrieking at him, "For crying out loud, Simon, will you please get out of bed already!" And he would throw the pillow off his face, slowly crawl out of the bed, and make his way to the bathroom, totally ignoring her. It was a rare morning when he got to school on time. By the time he left the house, my mother usually was so worn out that she landed back in her own bed.

My father's response was as scripted as my mother's. "Leave him alone, Ellen," he would urge her. "He'll get up on his own or he won't get up on his own. It doesn't matter what you do." But she never listened to him. Instead, she used all her energy screaming words Simon never heard, preparing a huge breakfast he never ate, and making threats she never kept.

I was so immune to the whole scene I hardly heard it anymore. My brother did, however, always save one remark to make me feel special before I left for school. "Did you stay up all night eating?" he might ask me. "You look a good ten pounds heavier than you did last night." Or "Good thing your nose is so big. Otherwise, that new zit would cover all of it." Or "Don't forget to bring a book to your soccer game today. You looked a little bored all alone on the bench yesterday." I struggled not to let his words hurt me, to listen to my mother when she said he didn't mean what he was saying, but it was hard to hold my head up and act like he hadn't sliced me into a million pieces. I *was* chubby. My skin *did* break out. I *was* a lousy soccer player.

Sometimes, I struggled to remember what our family life had been like before Simon had turned rotten. He had never been sweet or uncomplicated, but he hadn't always been so mean. That morning, while my mother was in the midst of her screaming routine, I sat on my bed and thought about one summer day nine years earlier. I had been six years old and Simon had been nine. We were swimming in the lake near my grandmother's summer home in New Hampshire. Our parents were on the shore, reading the newspaper. Our grandmother was setting up a picnic lunch. I was wearing a red bathing suit with black straps. I was a little chubby, but in the water I felt thin and loose and graceful. Simon was being mean to me. He'd called me fatso during breakfast, when I'd eaten four pieces of Nana's delicious cinnamon French toast. He'd said he hadn't brought a ball with him because his sister was a human beach ball. No one had said anything in my defense, and it had taken every bit of courage I had not to cry into the tiny blob of maple syrup on my empty plate.

Out in the water, however, I felt wonderful. Simon was a little farther out than I was. I reached down and felt the muddy bottom beneath me. I had taken swimming lessons at day camp earlier that summer and knew how to do the crawl, the breast stroke, and the side stroke. I wasn't a strong swimmer, but I wasn't bad. My parents had warned me not to go out over my head unless they were with me. I always listened to them, but that morning I felt strangely free. I could go out a little farther.

I looked down at my body and could see the outline of my red bathing suit beneath the dark water. I didn't look that fat. As soon as I started to do the crawl, I felt even thinner and more graceful. And then it hit me. A shooting pain in my right leg. My leg wouldn't move. Not one little bit. Before I knew what was happening, I was swallowing a huge gulp of lake water. All I could think about was that I wasn't a human beach ball. If I were, I wouldn't be sinking. I didn't want to sink. I wanted to get back on shore with my mother and father and grandmother. The taste of salt in my mouth was not from the lake water, which was never salty. I was crying. And drowning.

I heard my mother scream, and I began to cry harder. I tried very hard to move across the water, but the only direction I could go was downward—down, down, toward the mushy, gucky lake bottom. Suddenly, there was a strong arm against my chest and my head broke the surface of the water. I wanted to push the arm away before it could pull me farther toward the bottom, but the voice was so kind, I didn't fight it. "Hang on, Emmy," it said over and over. "I've got you, Sis. I'd never let anything happen to you."

"Oh, Simon," I whispered softly on my bed, so many years later. "Whatever happened to us all?"

"You are *so* lucky!" Carrie informed me later that day at lunch. "You have to take me with you to Sarah's. I have warts, too." She rolled up the right sleeve of her denim work shirt and pointed to the middle of her elbow. "See, I'm in terrible pain from this hideous wart. Please let me come. I promise, I'll be your very best friend in the whole world if you let me come."

"You already are my very best friend in the whole world," I reminded her. "And you always will be. I'll call my mother as soon as school's out and ask her. Okay?"

"Oh, no!" Carrie's face folded into a deep frown. "I can't go today. I just remembered. I have that stupid student council meeting. I can't believe my miserable luck."

I shook my head in disbelief. If Carrie Burns wasn't my best friend, I would hate her. Only wonderful things happened to her. No matter how hard she tried to belittle them, they were astounding. Like the student council meeting. She had been selected by both the student body and the faculty to represent our freshman class on the student council. Immediately, she'd volunteered to serve on the committee trying to combat the drinking problem in our school. The previous year, two RHS students, a junior and a senior, had been killed in separate drunk driving accidents. A sophomore, a junior, and two seniors had been admitted to drug rehab programs. And, one month before, the police had busted a huge wild party, painstakingly described by the *Boston Globe* and three local televisions stations, given by a Rockmere sophomore. Dozens of kids had attended, forty-two of whom had been arrested for being minors in possession. Our town was gaining a widespread reputation for having a terrible drinking problem in its high school, and the publicity was violently rocking quiet little Rockmere.

But my good buddy, freshman Carrie Burns, had constructed, all by herself, a plan to deal with the problem, a plan that had already won the support of many students and teachers and that she was about to present to the student council. She had spent countless hours on it, and I thought it was brilliant. It involved allowing the students the opportunity to police themselves, as well as proposing options for kids other than drinking. A lot of it revolved around a buddy system in which students would make a concerted effort to help their friends control their drinking. Guidance counselors would work with students, enacting situations involving drinking and constructive ways to handle it. There were other ideas that Carrie had not yet presented to anyone, but the best part of the whole proposal was that it recognized the fact that some students were going to drink no matter what anyone said or did. Instead of alienating those kids, Carrie's proposal included them and offered suggestions about safe drivers and support groups for kids worried about their friends' drinking habits.

"When your plan makes it through the student council," I told her, "you will be the new Rockmere witch and should be able to remove warts all by yourself."

"It's just never going to make it," she insisted. "I need at least another week to work out the details. Hey, I just thought of something. Carl O'Malley said I can't present it until we're done with other new business items. You'll be at Sarah Goody's house by then. How 'bout you ask her to give me a little zap during my presentation? You know, just to help me stay focused and on target. And maybe a little zap to the council so they'll listen to me. Will you do that?"

"Sure," I answered, trying to keep a straight face. "I'll make sure Sarah takes care of that before my wart."

Carrie leaned across the table and hugged me. "What would I ever do without you?" she asked. I didn't bother to answer.

At three o'clock that afternoon, while Carrie sat at the student council meeting and waited for her chance to solve the alcohol problems of every teenager in our town, I sat by my mother as she turned her white Volvo station wagon in at 13 Derby Street. Suddenly, the whole atmosphere changed. Eerily, the sun ducked behind a huge set of black clouds and the bright October sky turned dark and foreboding.

I'd given almost no thought to the whole witchy scene. Occasionally during the drive, I'd rubbed my finger against my wart and tried to imagine how Sarah would remove it. I expected her to utter some mumbo jumbo and sprinkle a few drops of cat blood on the wart, and then it would go away. But now I was feeling very shaky. The house itself actually didn't look that spooky. With its gables and black shingles, it looked like an ordinary historic Salem home—except for the brightly colored weird emblems decorating its windows. But between the increasingly dark sky and the wobbly feeling in my knees, I was thinking I just might stay in the car. "Hey, how about we get a frozen yogurt at the Salem Witch Creamery and forget my wart altogether?" I suggested. "I'm starved. And I kind of like my wart. It's like an old friend."

"Don't be silly," my mother said as she grabbed her notebook and pocketbook from the car seat and opened her door. "The wart's ugly. And Sarah's waiting for us." For the first time, I noticed that my mother was not wearing one of her interview suits. She was wearing something pretty simple and basic. A black skirt and black blazer. No big deal, except that she was also wearing a black silk shirt, black stockings, and black heels. All this on a woman who almost never wore black. My mother looked like a witch.

A miniature witch, I soon realized, as the rattling of chains concluded and the door to number 13 opened. "Do come in, ladies," an amazingly clear voice instructed, and I glanced inside to see a mountain of black crepe paper rustling eerily against the doorway. Sarah Goody was most certainly one tall witch, at least four inches taller than my 5'8" mother. I suspected Sarah's girth to be massive, but considering her full-length black taffeta gown, who could tell? There could have been two other witches inside her gown for all I knew. Her face was white, more like a ghost's than a witch's, its powdery appearance broken by gobs of light blue eye shadow, piles of black mascara, and a sharply painted, bright red mouth. The eyes were as black as the mane of thick hair cascading over her imposing shoulders.

My eyes somehow moved from her face to her chest. There, dangling between what were either two voluminous breasts or the heads of the other two witches lurking inside her gown, hung a bright gold necklace, so shiny that even in the dismal entrance hall it beamed sunlike onto the nearby walls. The pendant was a five-sided figure with ornate Greek letters across its face. It took every bit of self-control I had to keep my hands at my sides and not reach toward that enticing object.

"Won't you come in, Emily?" The witch was talking to me. I was certain she now understood that the daughter of her interviewer was brain-damaged. My mother had already walked into the living room and was sitting in a large black armchair. I mean, I think it was my mother. Mom always looked excited or annoyed or tired or happy. The woman in the black armchair looked like a statue, totally relaxed and peaceful. For a brief moment, I thought about escape, but the sound of door locks confirmed what I suspected: I was hopelessly trapped in a room with a jumbo witch and a smaller witch.

I sank into a seat and prepared to be turned into something witchy. Maybe a middle-sized chubby witch. Whatever was going to happen, I decided, I could handle it. After all, it wasn't as if I already had this fantastic life. Except for Carrie, I had few friends. I was the worst soccer player in the freshman class. My grades were nothing to rave about. I was a good fifteen pounds overweight. My hair kinked up no matter how hard I tried to keep it straight. And my brother made my home life a living hell. Life had already toughened me. I could handle whatever it was about to deal me.

When the black cat landed on my shoulder, I screamed so loudly a black sword fell off the wall, knocking over the two black candles on the table beside my black chair. I struggled to catch my breath while the smaller witch picked up the candles and sword, and the mega-size witch shooed the cat away. "Oh, Sabrina," Sarah Goody cooed. "You are such a little devil. You don't like cats, Emily?"

"Oh, God, no. I love cats," I gushed, anxious not to offend. "They're my favorite animals in the whole world." I glanced at my mother, who was putting the sword back on the wall, and read her expression perfectly.

What the devil is the matter with you? my mother's face was asking me. *You always preferred dogs to cats. You always said that cats were stupid and unaffectionate, while dogs were smart and lovable.*

"When I was a little girl," I continued, ignoring my mother, "we had this incredibly smart, affectionate cat named Mary. But she got pregnant so many times we—" It suddenly occurred to me that Sarah might be pregnant. That would explain her massive bulk. Chances were she was ready to deliver any second. Visions of *Rosemary's Baby* with Mia Farrow's hideous, devil-faced newborn baby flooded my mind.

Luckily, the woman who had once rocked me in my carriage remembered our relationship. "Oh, Emmy." She sighed. "I can't believe you still remember Mary. That's so sweet. I always thought you hated that cat."

"Oh, I simply cannot believe that Emily could hate a cat," Sarah said, and I smiled broadly at Sabrina, now stretched out on the rug a few feet away from me. The cat, however, was not smiling broadly back, and her hiss was not only unmistakable but clearly directed at me. "Well, let's get down to business, ladies," Sarah continued, ignoring Sabrina. "We have so much to take care of. But let's get the most important thing taken care of first. That wart certainly does need attention, Emily.''

I glanced at my right hand, which had been wrapped up in a tight little ball since I'd arrived. How the heck had she managed to see it? Before I had a chance to unclench my fist, Sarah had left her seat and retrieved the sword from its spot on the wall. For a big woman, she sure did move fast. The next thing I knew, the coffee table beside my chair was settled between me and Sarah. The two black candles were now lit, and their flames fluttered eerily in the suddenly dark room. Seconds later, the sword was out of its sheath; its sharp, sharp edge had been brushed against the candles; and my right hand was resting between Sarah's surprisingly delicate hands. Sarah rubbed her fingers along my wart, closed her eyes, and muttered a few unintelligible words. Then she raised the sword above her head with one hand and reached down into the V neck of her gown with the other.

I was too stunned to move or scream, but terrified as I was, I was fascinated with the beauty and grace of the ceremony. I couldn't even look at my mother. I figured she was probably still sitting in her trancelike condition, unaffected by the fact that her right-handed daughter would never play the piano again. I was so caught up in the scene that when Sarah pulled a large potato out of her gown, I wasn't surprised. For all I knew, she had an entire potato farm in there. Or maybe one hundred pounds of potato salad.

The rest of the ceremony went so quickly I could barely keep up with it, even though I was at the center. After she sang a few more verses of unintelligible rhyme, Sarah closed her eyes and, with one incredibly well directed hit, smashed the sword horizontally through the center of the potato. Then she rubbed both perfectly symmetrical pieces of the potato against my wart, did some more heavy mumbo jumbo, pressed the potato pieces together, and mumbled some more.

"Follow me, Emily," she said suddenly and clearly, standing up and leading the way out of the living room. In one swift motion, still holding the potato, she undid the locks, opened the door, and walked into her backyard. It was sort of pretty. There was a nice stretch of grass, a bright red-brick patio, three yellow lounge chairs, a covered barbecue, and lots of big trees, most of which had already lost their leaves. The sun had actually come back out, and I could feel its warmth on my shoulders and head. I was wondering whether Sarah did a lot of barbecuing in the summer and if maybe she had parties there with other witches when she grabbed my wrist. Before I knew what was happening, I was on my knees on the grass, beside Sarah, who was in the same position, only now she was holding a small shovel. In a flash, a hole was dug, the potato was placed in the hole, the hole was filled, a few more words were mumbled, and Sarah and I were back on our feet.

"That's that," Sarah informed me, rubbing her soiled hands against her black gown. "Tonight is the full moon. As the moon begins to wane during the next fourteen days, so will your wart. When the moon is at its smallest form, your wart will have disappeared."

"But the potato?" I asked. "What about it?"

"It will rot," she answered simply. "Like your wart."

My left hand touched my wart. Already, it felt weaker. For a moment, so did I. "Are you all right?"

Sarah asked as I swayed ever so slightly. "Do you need to sit down, Emily?"

"I'm fine," I said, noticing for the first time that my mother was in the backyard, too. She had her notebook out and was busy scribbling. I wondered, if I fainted would she write that down, too?

"Stand perfectly still, Emily," Sarah ordered me in a no-nonsense tone, moving in front of me. The woman was so large, it was as if a big black building had been placed in front of my body. I couldn't move if I wanted to. Once again, her eyes closed, convincing me that Sarah spent most of her waking hours with her eyes shut. The big arms and delicate fingers fluttered busily in front of me, circling my body as if they were fitting me for a full-length coat. Then the mumbo jumbo started again, big time. I thought I heard the word *Emily* muttered along with the rhymes, which were different from the ones that had accompanied the potato ceremony. Closer and closer came Sarah's arms, finally touching the crown of my head, the tops of my shoulder blades, the outlines of my hips and legs, and coming to rest at the tips of my shoes. This woman could move. She was hefty, but she was as graceful as a ballroom dancer. And for one long moment, I felt graceful, too—graceful and wonderfully safe.

"Well, that should take care of you," Sarah said while I stood there, feeling as if she had measured my body for a coat of armor. "I drew a protection shield around you that will eliminate those fainting spells. And defend you from other negative forces."

"Were there a lot of them?" my mother, the reporter-witch, asked casually, as if we were discussing a stranger we'd just met at a barbecue in Sarah's yard. This was the same woman who reacted hysterically if her daughter left for school without gloves on a warm day in April. "It seemed to take you much longer to do her than me."

"You got shielded?" I asked. "When? I thought you only got your tarot cards read yesterday."

"Oh, I thought I told you about the protective shield," she answered me, talking in a calm voice that didn't belong to my mother. "Sarah was concerned about some evil forces around me, too. But it took her only a few seconds to do me. You took at least ten times longer with Emily, didn't you, Sarah?"

"Yes," Sarah agreed. "Emily's field was more heavily populated. But don't worry. She'll be fine now."

"Good," the reporter-witch said. There was no way my *mother* could have heard about a field heavily populated with danger for her only daughter and merely responded with a "Good."

"So, how do you feel now, Emily?" Sarah asked as I stretched my shoulders and turned my head from side to side. I felt . . . strangely . . . good.

"Good," I answered. "Really good."

"That's wonderful," Sarah said, placing one of her hefty arms around my shoulders. "Well, I think we've done enough for one day, don't you?"

"Absolutely," I agreed. I noticed that Sarah looked a little tired. It was hard to tell because she wore so much makeup, but right around her eyes, even through the tons of mascara and eye shadow, I detected some weariness. I rubbed my wart. Man, it felt ready to rot. But the rest of me felt stronger and freer than ever before. "Thanks a million."

"You're very welcome," she said. "Please feel free to come back with your mother tomorrow when we do past life regressions."

"Sure," I said. "I just might."

"Don't you have a soccer game against Winthrop tomorrow?" my mother said, sounding a lot more like herself.

"Oh, yeah," I said. "But I could miss it. No one will care."

"Oh, really?" Sarah asked. "I suggest you go, Emily."

"Sure," I answered. Whatever she said was fine with me.

As we headed out of Sarah's kitchen, she reached for my mother's hand and shook it warmly. Her hand was so much bigger than my mother's that I got a little nervous that she might squash my mom's narrow fingers. But my mother seemed most comfortable with the handshake. "You take good care of yourself, Ellen," Sarah said once she gave my mother back her hand. "And be sure to call me later."

"I will, Sarah," my mother answered her. And the way the two of them smiled at each other, I could sense that they might be turning into friends. My mother had a lot of friends, but Sarah was certainly her first witch friend. I couldn't imagine the two of them shopping together or playing tennis or going to exercise class. Maybe they'd just be tea friends. Or potato friends. It was all quite beyond me.

After the two new friends had finally said good-bye to each other, my mother and I got back into her car. Once my mom backed her car out of the driveway at 13 Derby, I started to feel bad that all of her new friend's energies had gone into my life today. "Why didn't you have Sarah work on part two of your past lives regression series today?" I asked my mother as we licked our Heath Bar Crunch frozen yogurt cones from the Salem Witch Creamery. Usually, my mother insisted that we eat nonfat frozen yogurt, but that afternoon she ordered us regular, fattening yogurt as if we both ate it all the time. It was strange, but I was getting used to strange. "I know how excited you were about finding out if you were Cleopatra. We could have waited a few days for my potato ceremony. My finger wasn't in that much danger."

"No, but the rest of your body was," my mother said, licking away and driving. "Sarah felt she had no time to spare."

I stopped licking. "What are you talking about? Those little spells were nothing to worry about. I've never once fainted."

"That's not it, Emmy," she said. "I told you Sarah was worried about someone in our family. When I called her to ask if you could get your wart done one of these days, she told me to bring you immediately. She wouldn't tell me anything else, except that she would fix whatever was wrong. And she did."

Slowly, I began to lick again. But the Heath Bar Crunch frozen yogurt had lost its delicious taste. Something really weird was going on. Part of me thought my visit to Sarah's house had been the stupidest thing in the world. My mother was writing a Halloween story about the witch, and I was helping her out. But another part of me wasn't sure. My wart was rotting. I just knew it. And I felt stronger and safer than I ever had. There was nothing imaginary about that.

"I'm sure I was Joan of Arc," my mother announced as we drove out of Salem. "I've been feeling very warm lately. Even on cool days. It's the flames. They're coming back. Plus you know how good I look with my hair short. I can't decide whether to get my bangs straightened or cut it all off. What do you think?''

I thought my mother might be experiencing hot flashes. Or senility. But I looked at her carefully. She was right. She did look terrific with short hair. And she'd forgotten something important. She'd been an award-winning equestrian in high school. If I had to bet, I'd put all my pennies on Joan of Arc.

four
4

I felt sick with guilt when I spoke to Carrie that night. "Even your zap didn't help me," she sobbed over the phone. "I lost by one vote. Arlene Peterson said she just couldn't vote for my proposal, that it didn't sound well thought out. She didn't mean to be mean, just honest. And she was right. I hadn't thought everything out. And she had some ideas that were far better than mine."

"Don't be so hard on yourself," I said. "You'll have another chance with them. Next time, I'm sure you'll get every point across perfectly."

"No, I won't," she insisted. "I'm just fooling myself, Emily. I want the glory of solving the drinking problems of the whole town. My plan was too unrealistic. Arlene's was sensible. I need to take a back seat and let her be in charge. And that makes me feel awful."

I was clueless about how to handle this situation. For the past nine years, our relationship had been organized around the premise that I did everything wrong and she did everything right. Now, for the first time, she was in terrible pain, and I didn't know how to help her. Plus I felt so guilty I wanted to die. I had forgotten to ask Sarah to zap Carrie during her presentation. And I didn't even have the courage to tell Carrie the truth.

"You just have to work on it a little more," I told her instead. "And go back and make them listen. Arlene Peterson is a dimwit. There's no way any plan she could come up with would be better than yours. Your ideas are so terrific, Carrie. You owe it to the school to try again. There's too much at stake to bury your head in the sand because a few idiots didn't listen to you. Promise me you won't abandon everyone because of them."

There was silence on the phone. Finally, Carrie answered me. "You're right, Emmy," she said, her sobs beginning to subside. "I won't give up. Thanks for making me see that. But can I ask you one more favor?"

"Of course. Anything."

"Will you ask Sarah Goody to give me a stronger zap next Monday at two-thirty in the afternoon? I think I need more than your usual zap."

"No problem," I said. "I was supposed to go back there tomorrow to hear about my mom's past lives, but we have that stupid soccer game against Winthrop."

"You're giving *that* up for a soccer game?" Carrie sounded dumbfounded. "I can't believe you."

"You think I shouldn't go to the game?" I asked.

"Not really," she answered. "I'm just surprised you're going to the game rather than to Sarah's, that's all."

"Because I'm so lousy, right?"

"No. You're not lousy. You just don't enjoy it."

"Is that my only problem?" I asked. "I don't enjoy it?"

"That's not what I meant," she said.

"Maybe not," I said. "But tell me this. If I start to enjoy it more, will I do better?"

"Sure," she said.

"Thanks," I said. I felt as if Carrie had given me a gift. The truth was, I wanted to enjoy soccer. I didn't care if I was as good as she was. I saw the way the other girls ran around the field during our practices. While I kept my eye on my watch, counting the seconds until I could limp off the field, they were all hooting and laughing, sweating and letting their hair go wild, having a great time chasing the ball through the grass. I wanted to be loose like they were, but I just didn't feel like part of the team. All of them were real athletes; I was the pretender, the klutz who had snuck onto the team because her mother wrote a great story about girls' sports for the local newspaper.

Winthrop was the strongest team in our division. Our record was three and two, and if we were going to make it to the conference finals, we had to beat Winthrop. The next day, I met Carrie at her locker before the game, and we walked to the field together. Jessica Francis joined us as soon as we approached the soccer field. "Big game, huh, Carrie?" she said, ignoring me as always. "Man, do we need to kick some serious butt today."

Jessica makes me sick. It's not just that she's tall and pretty and looks like a teenage Julia Roberts, it's her attitude. She thinks she's just so terrific. Every time she walks off the soccer field, she has this smile on her face that just screams out "Wasn't I incredible!" She's about 5'10" and has really strong legs and arms. Of course, she's a natural on the soccer field. Sometimes, she's sort of nice to me because she knows I'm Carrie's best friend and, like everybody on the team—and probably the whole world—she loves Carrie. But I know she can't stand me. I've seen her face when the coach sends me in. She wants to puke.

"I know, Jess," Carrie agreed. "But what about your knee? I know it was bothering you our last game."

"It's a little better," Jessica said. "My mom brought me to the doctor yesterday and he said I should apply ice to it after practice. Hey, that reminds me." She turned to me and smiled. "I saw your brother while I was waiting for my mom to pick me up for my appointment. Is he still going with Barby Gold?"

"I'm not sure," I answered.

"Well, let me know if you hear they've split. He is so gorgeous." I saw how she was looking at me. *And you are so ugly,* she was saying silently. "So, you think he's still going with Barby?" she asked aloud.

"I'm not sure," I repeated.

"I don't think so," Carrie said. "I heard they had a huge fight last weekend."

"Oh, yeah," I agreed, although I had no idea whether my brother was still going out with Barby Gold. Or Alicia Silverstone. "I guess they did."

"Well, he was totally flirting with me yesterday," Jessica said. "Be sure and tell him to feel free to call me. Any time."

"Let's concentrate on our game," Carrie said as we reached the field. She didn't seem the least bit happy with the thought that Jessica and my brother could get it together. Poor Carrie. She was wasting her time thinking about Simon. She was so great and he was such a loser. She could have any guy she wanted. I saw the way Brian always looked at her. He was hers for the asking. But she didn't seem to be that interested in him. How could she want Simon rather than Brian?

The game was unbelievable. We were tied two all in the final period with two minutes left when Coach Goldstein put me in. I almost died. She never put me in when we were tied. But I sort of knew why she was doing it. In practice, I'd been good. I don't know what had gotten into me, but I was moving around the field, and Carrie saw that and kept feeding me the ball. And I kept kicking it and running around, almost like I was having fun and was a genuine member of the team. "Way to go, Emmy!" Carrie screamed every time I touched the ball. She had been so excited that I kept going just to make her happy.

Of course, when the whistle blew and the real game began, I slunk back to the bench, perfectly content to watch the real players take over. Well, I did feel a twinge of regret, but I swallowed it quickly and reminded myself who I was: the worst player on the team in spite of one decent practice. But when Alexandra Stern sprained her ankle and Carol Wayne got stomach pains, Coach Goldstein called my name, and the next thing I knew I was up there with the forwards, chasing that big black-and-white ball all over the field. "Way to go, Emmy baby!" Carrie kept shouting, and even Jessica yelled an encouraging "Nice boot!" when I connected with the ball for a short kick.

There was no doubt the Winthrop girls were huge. Bigger than anyone on our team. Unfortunately, I have this fear about collisions, which is not a good thing for a soccer player to have. I was always impressed with the way Carrie would dive into a group of opponents, never giving her own safety a thought.

She was out there for one purpose only: to get that ball into the opposing net. And if it meant she was going to lose a limb or a few teeth, so be it. But that afternoon against Winthrop, I felt fearless, as if I could put my body in front of any opposing player and not worry. I nearly had a heart attack when Coach Goldstein got up and started to call me off the field. I mumbled a quick prayer that she would fall down and leave me alone, and sure enough, she banged into the end of the bench and fell on her butt. So when the miracle happened, and I kicked the ball into the Winthrop net with three seconds left on the clock, I wasn't even thinking about breaking my nose. All I was thinking was "This is fun."

The first player to hug me was Jessica. Her long arms clenched me so tightly I could barely breathe. "I always knew you could do it, Emmy!" she shouted into my ear. I was thrilled, but I wasn't brain-dead. I knew Jessica Francis had never always known I could do it. But I smiled merrily and shook my head in agreement.

"You're having fun, aren't you?" Carrie yelled as we jumped up and down, our arms wrapped around each other. "You're finally having fun out here!"

When the last three seconds ended and I walked off the field, Coach Goldstein shook my hand. "I couldn't believe the way you deflected that huge full-back coming at you just before you kicked," she said. "I was sure that monster was going to level you, but you held your ground. And she hit the dirt. You're one tough lady, Emily."

"Did you see the fullback who nearly toppled me?" I asked Carrie as we walked home. She honestly seemed happier with my success than when she scored the winning goal herself. "Coach Goldstein told me about her, but I swear I didn't see her."

"I don't know how you could have missed her," Carrie said. "She weighed about three hundred pounds, and was ten feet tall with legs like tree trunks."

"Seriously, Carrie, I didn't see her."

"That's amazing," Carrie said. "She had flaming red hair that was all over her face. You really didn't see her?"

I thought hard. I did remember a big body or two around, but it was almost as if I had blinders on. All I could see was the ball. And coach's falling on her rear . . . "Guess not," I said.

"Well, I wouldn't worry about her if I were you," Carrie said. "Because you heard the music, kid, and those feet began to dance." She hugged me for the hundredth time. "And I am *so* proud of you!" She was dying to come inside and tell my mother about the game, but I convinced her I would handle the bragging just fine. "I'll check that out myself when I call you tonight!" she yelled before disappearing down the street.

My mother was sitting at the kitchen table when I walked into the house; she was wearing a black skirt, a black sweater, black tights, and black shoes. She even wore black earrings. "Guess what?" I said. "You will not believe what happened at my soccer game."

My mother looked up from the book she was reading. It was titled *Sonnets from the Portuguese*. Her eyes were filled with tears. "Oh, Emmy," she said softly, "you must listen to this poem. Sit down, please." I sat. I wanted to tell her about the most incredible moment in my life, but instead I sat and listened quietly while she read.

> *How do I love thee? Let me count the ways.*
> *I love thee to the depth and breadth of light*
> *My soul can reach, when feeling out of sight*
> *For the ends of being and ideal grace.*

Tears streamed down my mother's face as she read the entire poem. As she read and wept, I noticed she was wearing weird makeup; it was sort of white. "Isn't that the most beautiful poem you have ever heard in your whole life?" my mother asked. I nodded. It was kind of sweet and slightly familiar. "I wrote it for Robert," she told me. "Years and years ago."

"Robert?" I asked. "Who's he?" She continued to stare at the poem. I wasn't sure she'd heard me. "You wrote that?" I asked, speaking louder this time. "You're kidding. I thought it was some famous poem."

"It is famous," she admitted, looking up at me. "But I wrote it for my beloved husband, Robert. In my other life, of course. I was Elizabeth Barrett Browning then."

She was making me good and nervous the way she was talking, and she still had tears in her eyes. "Oh, Sarah did your past life regression," I finally remembered. "And you were a poet, huh? That's nice. What happened to Cleopatra and Joan of Arc?"

"They didn't come out today," she told me. "They may come out another time, but Elizabeth just jumped right out the second Sarah brought me back. I was an invalid, you know. I had a spinal cord injury, but Robert carried me away from my overprotective father's home in London and brought me to Italy. I was very pale and small, as pure as my poetry. Robert and I were married in 1846 and were deliciously happy together in Italy until my death in 1861.''

I'd never thought of my mother as pale and small, but I did have to admit that, hunched over the book of poetry, her face covered with white makeup, she looked exceptionally pale and small. "I think I need to lie down for a few minutes," she told me as she stood up very carefully, as if walking were a painful endeavor. "Can you help me upstairs?"

"Ma!" I screamed so loudly the poor little pale and black thing nearly collapsed. "What is going on here? You're a reporter writing a story about a witch! Stop clowning around. You're acting crazy."

My voice must have had the same magical powers as my soccer foot, because the pale and small lady disappeared and my mother, albeit with the black clothes and white makeup, reappeared. "Sorry, honey," she said, standing up straight now. "But that poetry got to me. You have to remember, I wrote my master's thesis on Victorian poetry, so I've always had the heart and soul of a poet. I'm not surprised to find out I was Elizabeth Barrett Browning. It's a perfect match."

"Yeah, that's nice," I said, "but I made a perfect match myself today. With a soccer ball. I scored the winning goal against Winthrop today."

The creature in black acted just the way my mother would. She jumped up and down, insisting she'd known all along that I was a talented soccer player, and covered me with kisses and hugs. When she put a brand-new black apron over her black skirt and read me one more poem before she began to make dinner,

I got a tiny bit nervous. But when she ripped the bag of Oreos out of my hand before I got even one tiny crumb, I knew Elizabeth was back in Italy and Mom was right there in Rockmere.

five

*W*hen Simon didn't come home for dinner that night, none of us was that concerned. For the past two years, ever since he got his license, it was no big deal for him to come home around nine or ten, ignoring my mother's questions and tuning out my father's anger. Sometimes he'd offer an excuse, like he'd been working on a friend's car or had gone to a movie and ended up staying for a second feature. He never called to say he'd be late. It seemed as if my parents had decided it wasn't worth making a big fuss over, even if he reeked of alcohol or carried the faint smell of marijuana. He was home; he hadn't been arrested or wrecked his car or ended up in an emergency room.

But when it was time for the eleven o'clock news and he still wasn't home, my parents got nervous. After they called two of his friends, Bobby Kane and Mike Richmond, and found out Simon had left school after lunch, they got more tense. "It's not like he's never skipped an afternoon of classes," my father said, trying to rationalize.

I'm not a psychiatrist, but I've never had any trouble seeing that even though my mother is the most vocal about Simon and ends up having the worst screaming sessions with him, it's my father whose heart has been crushed the most by him. My mother always manages to convince herself that somehow Simon will turn out okay. My father surrendered that hope, probably around two years before, when Simon got to be so much more difficult to handle, and it shows.

Once, in the midst of an especially hideous scene, my brother had shouted "Just my rotten luck to have gotten adopted by a crazy mother and a pathetic father!"

The adoption thing had never come up before during a fight. We all thought about it, but no one ever verbalized it. My mother looked like she was going to pass out, but my father hung tight. "She was perfectly sane when I married her," he'd told my brother in a clear, calm voice. "And so were you when you made us a family. But life has a funny way of making us all crazy, doesn't it?" Simon had stared at my father for a minute, then he'd run out of the room. It was one of those rare times when a scene with Simon didn't leave my parents not talking to one another. My father still had some hope left then, but that was a long time ago.

"Oh, really?" My mother's voice brought me back to the present. "Well, in case you're interested, Simon hasn't cut a class in over four weeks. His guidance counselor told me he said it wasn't worth the hassle of detention. Plus, he was in an exceptionally good mood when he left the house this morning. He asked me to make him a lunch and was very grateful when I did."

I wanted to puke. If I ask for a lunch, my mother tells me to make my own. But he not only got his made, he got extra credit for having asked in a decent manner. Oh, brother.

"Well, that is unusual," my father agreed. "But doesn't it also sound a bit unusual that he asked for a lunch and then left school *after* lunch?"

"No," she said. "Why?"

"I don't know," my father said. "It sounds funny to me."

"I'd rather dwell on where he is right now, rather than what he ate for lunch," my mother said. "Where do you think he went, Emily? Did any of your friends mention him at school today?"

"Jessica from my soccer team was talking about him," I told her. I could see the desperation building in her eyes and I knew I had to offer her something.

"Oh, really." She brightened a little bit. "And what did she say?"

"Just that he was good-looking and she'd heard he'd broken up with Barby Gold."

"Maybe we should call Barby," my mother said. "Maybe they got back together and he's with her. Do you think it's too late for you to call her, Emmy?"

"Me?" I asked. "Why do I have to call her?"

"Because you're looking for your brother," she pleaded. "Please do me this favor and call her."

"I know it's a pain," my father said. "But your mother could be right. He could be trying to set things straight with Barby."

There was nothing I could do to get out of this one. They'd both be on my case all night long if I didn't make the call. I knew I might as well do it and get it over with already. Barby Gold answered her phone on the first ring. "Simon and I broke up last week," she informed me when I asked her if Simon might be there. I hated the way she spoke, like she had a potato in her mouth. She was pretty smart and probably would end up going to a top college after graduation, but there had to be something wrong with her if she had gone out with my brother for a while. I didn't care how good-looking he was; any normal girl would realize how bad he was in no time.

"Oh, I'm sorry to hear that," I said, feeling stupid to have called her.

"Don't be," she said. "It's no big deal. But if you're wondering where he is, I can tell you."

"Thanks," I said while she finished putting red polish on her last toenail. Don't ask me how I knew this, but I was certain she was sitting on her bed painting her toenails red.

"Mike Richmond told me Simon was heading up to New Hampshire to get some alcohol for the Halloween dance," she told me as she put the cover on the bottle of nail polish.

"Thanks for the info," I told her, trying to act cool even though I was getting a stomachache. Poor Carrie was so desperate to keep the dance alcohol-free. How could she possibly like my brother? They were as different as night and day. I dreaded telling her he and Barby were through. But she was my best friend. I had no choice but to give her what she would consider fantastic news. "I'm sure he'll be home any minute. Sorry I bothered you."

"No problem," Barby said. "See you around."

I told my parents that Barby Gold and Simon had broken up and she had no idea where he was. They looked sad; my father went to bed and my mother went into her study. I called Carrie and told her that Barby Gold and Simon had broken up, and she squealed with excitement. And then she went back to work on a new plan to keep the dance alcohol-free. I knew the only plan that would work would be to chloroform my brother for a year, but I said nothing.

I went to bed at midnight. I had a math test the next day, and I knew how poorly I'd do if I was tired, especially if there were word problems. But once I got into bed, I couldn't sleep. I kept thinking about Jessica Francis's making such a fuss about running into Simon, like he was such a big deal just because he was good-looking. And poor Carrie. There were so many guys who would die to go out with her, but the one she dreamed about was Simon the loser. And why was he still out when he'd just gone to New Hampshire? Nothing about Simon was ever normal and easy, but this latest scene seemed even more abnormal than usual. I must have fallen asleep, because the next thing I knew the clock read 3 A.M. I got out of bed and walked into my brother's room. There he was, sound asleep under his covers, looking as innocent as any normal guy. I sighed and was heading back to my room when I noticed the light on in my mother's study. She was sitting at her desk, not writing, just staring at the wall beyond her desk. She was still wearing the same black outfit she'd worn when I'd gone to sleep.

"When did he get home?" I asked quietly, hoping I wouldn't frighten her.

"Oh, honey, what are you doing up?" she asked me.

"When did he get home?" I asked her again.

"An hour ago. I came in to tell you but you were sleeping. I didn't want you to worry all night about him."

"Well, now you can get to sleep, too."

She didn't move from her chair. "Yup," she said. "It's a big relief."

"You don't seem relieved," I said.

"I'm fine," she said. "Not that I have any idea where he was, but at least he's home. I'm just going to sit here for a minute now. But I want you to go back to sleep."

"Please tell me why you're still worried," I said. I couldn't bear to leave her like that. Usually, once Simon came home she'd go right to bed, as if she was saving her strength for the inevitable scene in the morning. "It's Sarah, isn't it?" She nodded. I don't know how I knew, but I was positive she was upset about something to do with Sarah.

She sighed and looked directly at me. "She said something might happen to someone in our family. You heard her say that."

"Come on, Mom," I said. "Don't start giving this lady big powers. She makes a lot of guesses and sometimes she's right and sometimes she isn't. Every one of us is in danger. Life is dangerous."

My mother looked like she was going to cry. Man, I wished I knew some Elizabeth Barrett Browning poetry that could snap her out of it, but I didn't know any poems at all. "Of course, I know that," she said, "but I'm just so worried about all of us. Sure, Simon's home now, but God only knows what he'll get into tomorrow. And I'm worried about you. And your father. I just feel so fearful, like something awful is about to happen. This time, we escaped. Simon's home. But I'm just so frightened about next time."

"We've got our protective shields," I reminded her, trying to sound lighthearted but finding it difficult to stay awake.

"Hey, this is silly," my mother finally admitted, standing up and putting an arm around my shoulders. "Enough craziness. You look ready to collapse. Go to sleep already. You've got a big math test in the morning, in case you've forgotten.''

I hadn't forgotten. Any more than I had forgotten that weird look on Sarah Goody's face when she drew the protective shield around me. My mother was right. Something awful was about to happen. I wasn't certain exactly what it was, but it had to do with both Simon and me. I just prayed that the shield Sarah had given me didn't have a hole in it.

School was unbelievable the next day. First, I aced the math test, which was all word problems. I'd simply look at a problem, like how long it would take a speeding locomotive to get from Oregon to Maryland, and instead of getting my usual math-induced headache, I'd get an answer. Never before had I finished a math test before the allotted time, but that morning I was done less than thirty minutes into the fifty-minute period.

Ms. Madorsky looked as surprised as I must have. The first thing she did was glance at my paper, certain I had just given up and was passing in an incomplete exam. I could see the look, a mixture of pity and frustration. She was a nice teacher and spent a lot of time trying to make every student understand. I never understood math, not even when she went over things two or three times in class. I'd just get so nervous that I was holding up the class that my mind would go totally blank. In the privacy of my own room, sometimes I could make myself understand what she'd been teaching, but math was never easy for me.

That day, Ms. Madorsky didn't look frustrated or full of pity. She looked shocked. Her eyes raced to my desk. I couldn't blame her for thinking I'd cheated. But, as always, I'd been seated between Mary Ellen Lowry and James Finn, the three of us perpetually locked in the cellar of our class's test scale. "Nice work, Emily," Ms. Madorsky finally said as she checked my answers a second time. "Really, really nice work." I nodded and smiled and headed back to my seat. Mary Ellen and James both looked up at me as I skidded back into my seat and started gathering up my books. I hated to tell them, but if by some miracle things continued the way they were heading today, they would have a lot more room in the cellar from now on.

English class was just as exciting. And unusual. We were discussing Othello and his love for Desdemona. I'd been having a lot of trouble with Shakespeare. It drove me crazy that he used so many words that I didn't understand. Mr. Braunstein had given us a book that sort of translated Shakespeare. It didn't exactly put *Othello* in everyday English, but it made it a lot easier to understand. I'd read a couple of chapters during study period and came into class feeling a lot better about the whole Othello-Desdemona-Iago scene. When Mr. Braunstein brought up the subject of jealousy for about the thousandth time, I saw a whole new image. "Othello reminds me of O.J. Simpson," I volunteered. "I mean, here is a black man, a warrior who makes his living by being strong and defeating his opponents, married to a white woman who's a lot younger than he is. And he kills her because he thinks she's fooling around with his buddy Cassio. Othello seems like a nicer guy than O.J. and he kills her gently, but still he kills her. And that whole thing with her handkerchief could sort of be compared to O.J.'s bloody glove. You know, how did it get there in the first place? I wonder if O.J. reads a lot of Shakespeare.''

I don't speak up much in English, so it was a big deal for me to have said all that. Carrie was sitting next to me, and she started comparing Desdemona's handmaiden, Emilia, to Denise Brown and how they both tried unsuccessfully to save their mistress's or sister's life. I didn't really agree since Denise didn't do all *that* much to try to save her sister, but Carrie was really into it, so I let it go. I couldn't get over how much clearer everything in that play looked to me, like I was a critic, able to think of abstract themes and meanings.

At lunch, everyone was talking about my incredible goal in soccer, and at soccer practice, wherever the ball went, my foot was there. I'd always thought of Carrie as the fastest creature on the face of the earth, but I can't tell you how many times I got to the ball before her. I was beginning to worry that she spent too much time hugging and congratulating me. Maybe it was slowing her down.

It wasn't till I got home from school that I remembered Simon's latest escapade. If he'd really gone to New Hampshire, all the liquor he'd bought was going to screw up my brother, my best friend, the Halloween dance, and our family. But what amazed me was my reaction to this latest problem. When something was going on with Simon, it destroyed my whole school day. I was unable to concentrate and sometimes even went home sick. But that day, I never thought about Simon until I walked in the front door and saw my mother, the woman in black, sitting at her word processor, working on her Sarah Goody story. The desk in her little office off the kitchen was covered with books on Salem's history and witchcraft. She was always sort of scattered and messy when she was in the midst of a story, but that day she seemed exceptionally disorganized.

"Thank heavens you're home," she said before I had a chance to tell her one of the terrific things that had happened to me at school. "You've got to call Sarah for me right away."

"Haven't you seen her already today?" I asked, sitting down on the red-and-white couch in her office. When I was little, I used to lie on that couch while my mother wrote her stories, lulled by the steady tapping of her computer keys. Today she wasn't typing at all, just leafing through books and magazine articles. And looking harried.

My mother shook her head and gave me a sad smile. "No," she answered me. "I tried, but she was busy doing a hands-on healing at the hospital. Then some guy called to tell me to phone her the minute you got home. Apparently, she wants us to come to her house before five o'clock this afternoon. Well, actually, she wants *you* to come to her house at five. I'm to drive you and come back to pick you up."

"That's the dumbest thing I ever heard," I said. "Why, all of a sudden, am I the family representative to the witch's house? You're the one doing the story on her. And who's her male secretary? It doesn't make any sense."

"I agree," she said. "But that was her message. Maybe she's worried about your wart. Look, I don't know what's going on, but I'm sure it all has to do with Simon and his getting into some new mess. He was happy before he left for school, and considering how little sleep he got last night, that has to mean he's up to no good. Maybe Sarah can help us. Maybe she can draw him a protection shield. Maybe I'm losing my mind. I don't know. But there's something about this woman I really like, and I think it would be very interesting if you went to see her. If nothing else, you'll come home with something for my story. What do you have to lose? A wart?''

I looked at my mother for a few minutes, trying to determine if she was joking. It was hard to tell. Mostly, she looked tired. I looked at my watch. It was a quarter to five already. "Get the broomstick ready," I told her, reaching for the phone. "It's time to fly."

She didn't smile at that one. Instead, she sat still while I called Sarah's house and told some guy with a deep voice that my mother and I were on the way. Then she closed the books on her desk, grabbed her pocketbook, and led the way to the garage. She didn't argue when I insisted that we stop at Salem Witch Creamery for a quick scoop. It was amazing what powers I now had. It was only when I was eating my Coffee Heath Bar yogurt that I realized I might be a little thinner than usual. My jeans were looser than normal. It must have been all that running around the soccer field, I decided. As my mother backed out of the creamery parking lot, I stole a glance in her rear-view mirror. A kind of perky, not-too-bad-looking girl looked back at me. I put some of her shiny, not frizzy, hair behind her ears and wondered for a second what on earth was happening here.

Knocking at the door of 13 Derby Street, however, I was only wondering one thing: How had I ever let Mom convince me I had to go visit this witch alone? It was one thing to go there with my mother, but no matter how thin and cute I felt, I didn't want to spend time alone in a witch's house.

My mom took off after promising to be back in a half hour, and I rang Sarah's doorbell and wished I were anywhere else. When five minutes went by and no one came to the door, I began to feel a little hopeful. Maybe Sarah had to go out for an emergency. Maybe somebody needed an immediate past life regression and she'd had to take off to the library to figure out what country he'd been king of. Or maybe she was just out in the backyard, checking on my potato plant. I was studying my reflection in the glass part of her front door when the door suddenly opened. The cutest guy I have ever seen in my life said, "Come in, Emily."

Now, understand that I'm Simon's sister, and the whole world seems to agree that Simon is movie-star-quality good-looking. "If the world didn't fawn all over him," my mother's said a million times, "then he wouldn't have such a tough time making his way out there." One incident that proves her point happened when Simon was ten and I was seven, and we'd gone to get candy bars at our neighborhood grocery store. The lady at the cash register, who looked old enough to be our mother, handed Simon a piece of paper which he read out loud as we walked home. "Call me anytime," the note had read. "We'll have some fun together. Lori, 631-5692." My mother had nearly died when Simon showed her the note and had marched herself off to the grocery store to confront the cashier, who was then fired. But she was just one of countless women who'd since thrown themselves at my brother's feet.

But this guy in Sarah's doorway had Simon beat by a mile. It took every bit of strength I had to stand up straight and walk through the door. I wanted to speak, to let this Greek god know I was available and in love with him, but all I could do was smile idiotically. Gorgeous didn't seem to mind my idiocy at all.

As a matter of fact, he offered me the same smile I'd seen so many guys bestow on Carrie. "Sarah's tied up for a few minutes," he told me. "Why don't you come into the den and we'll wait till she's through?"

He led the way into the den, which was as scary as the living room, with candles and black furniture and heavy black velvet drapes. There were pictures on the walls of weird-looking people in black suits and long black dresses. With this handsome creature at my side, though, the room seemed filled with sunlight.

"Can I get you a cold drink or anything?" he asked me, standing so close I could feel the soft, shiny fabric of his black pants against my jeans. He was also wearing a plain black sweatshirt and black sneakers with no socks. I didn't mean to look so closely, but there was no way my eyes were going to stay off this guy's face or body. "A Coke or some tea?" Before I could answer, he walked over to an end table and poured me a cup of tea. I'd stared at guys' butts before, but never had I seen one as fetching as his.

"No," I answered as I took the cup he handed me. I'm not a big tea drinker, but the scent from this tea was beyond delicious, kind of a combination of licorice and roses. I only meant to take a sip, but I emptied the cup in one long, scrumptious swallow. "I'm fine. Just fine. I'm Emily Silver."

He smiled, revealing a gorgeous set of pearly whites that made even Simon's perfect smile look like matchsticks, took my empty teacup out of my hands, and placed it back on the table. I tried to guess his age, but my mind drew a blank. His face looked young and old at the same time. The only age I could come up with was somewhere between eighteen and twenty-two. There was something weird about him, I knew, but normal didn't seem all that appealing to me at that moment. "I know," he said, sitting down on the black couch and patting the spot next to him. "I've been waiting for you. I'm Jeremiah Brooks. Sarah's son."

"Oh," I said, trying to sit down gracefully. The seat was so low and so soft that I was practically swallowed up in leather. Jeremiah, being taller, seemed to have no such problem. "How nice to have a mother who's a witch. I have an aunt who's a doctor. Obstetrician-gynecologist. She's not married." The minute I said those words I wished I could have cut out my tongue. It was amazing how many stupid things I could fit into one brief statement.

"That's interesting," he said, smiling so nicely I decided it was a good thing my tongue was still in my mouth. Who knew what use I might want to make of it someday? "I'm especially interested in the medical profession. Sarah's actually in the midst of surgery right now. It's taking a little longer than she expected."

"Oh, I heard she was doing a healing at the hospital," I said, struggling to sit up. "I thought she'd be back by now. Guess her patient needed more healing, huh?" I hated the way I was sounding. So jerky and dumb. I was repulsing myself with the way I was reacting to hunky Jeremiah Brooks. I took a deep breath and tried again before he answered my stupid question. "Actually, I can imagine that healings often require more hands-on than one would think." I closed my mouth before I got any stupider, just in case that could possibly happen.

"She's not at the hospital," Jeremiah informed me. He was smiling nicely at me and didn't seem the least bit bothered by my stupidity. As a matter of fact, he seemed to accept every word I spoke as if it were fascinating. Either I'd totally lost my grasp on reality or this guy liked me. "She's here."

"She's operating here!" I sat upright in the couch for about a second before the thick leather ate me up again. "Where?"

"In the living room." He glanced at his watch. "Actually, the operation started over four hours ago and should be over any minute now."

"What kind of operation is she doing?" I asked. "Wart surgery?"

The smile just didn't fade. Not one bit. If anything, it deepened and showed two heavenly dimples. "No. Actually, it's a triple bypass. On a sixty-three-year-old male in California."

I gave up. "Oh," I said simply. There was no way I was going to figure this out. I was attractive to this hunk. Sarah was a cardiac surgeon who operated in her living room. Okay. "Nice. She went to California to operate on a guy's heart. Very nice."

"I know it's confusing, Emily," Jeremiah said patiently. "You see, it's an out-of-body experience. An OBE, if you will. Her astral body, sort of her body of Talking Sense, has been projected away from her physical body. My mother has left that physical body here, but she's traveled spiritually to California, where she's assisting in the surgery. She's helping the patient survive the psychic rigors of the operation, supplying him with the energy he needs to recover. And I must tell you, he's doing far better than any of us expected."

I forced myself into a total sitting position. "Let me make sure I've got this straight," I said. "Your mom had an OBE that let her go to California, where she got into an operating room and helped a surgeon perform a bypass?'' Jeremiah nodded. ''Does she do this often?'' I asked.

''At least once a month,'' he answered me. ''But, listen, she very much wants to see you, so please, just sit here and I'll go see if she's ready for you.''

He got up from the couch and took off for the hospital or whatever place Sarah was operating in, leaving me alone in the black room, whose sunlight disappeared with Jeremiah. He'd been gone only a few seconds when he reappeared. ''She's all set for you,'' he informed me, and helped pull me out of the leather couch. I felt surprisingly graceful and light as he lifted me to my feet and led the way into the living room.

Sarah was sitting in a big chair beside a small table on which five black candles were burning. Her eyes were closed and she looked like she was sleeping. I wasn't sure if it was my imagination or the dim light in the room, but Sarah didn't look quite as huge as she had the first time I saw her. Actually, she looked kind of pretty, sitting there with her eyes closed and her hands folded daintily in her lap. Her black hair seemed softer, and the white makeup wasn't as shocking. ''Mother,'' Jeremiah said softly and tenderly, leaning over the sleeping body and gently touching her shoulder. ''Emily's here.''

Sarah slowly opened her eyes and stared at me. For a moment, she didn't seem to have any idea who I was. She closed her eyes again and was breathing pretty heavily. Then, as if someone had pressed a switch, she opened her eyes, sat upright in the seat, and smiled warmly at me. ''Hi, Emily,'' she greeted me, reaching out her hand to shake mine. ''Forgive me. I've just been through an exhausting procedure. But I'm fine now.''

"Jeremiah told me about it," I said, shaking her hand. "How did the patient do?"

"He's fine," she told me. "Just fine. I'll go back there in an hour or so to supply him with some more strength, but for now he's doing wonderfully. But that's not what I wanted to speak to you about. Please take a seat, so you and I can get on with our business."

I sat down in a black love seat opposite her. Jeremiah sat beside me, so close our bodies were completely touching. "Is it about my wart?" I asked. I hated to talk about such a gross thing, but I felt as if Jeremiah and I shouldn't have any secrets. " 'Cause it's still there."

"Oh, it'll take a little while for that to disappear," Sarah told me. "But that's not what I wanted to talk about. It's your brother, Simon. He's in a lot of danger. I don't want your mother to know because there's nothing she can do about it."

"Wow," I said. "That's terrible. Don't you think she should know so she can tell the police?"

"I think I can do more to help your brother than the police," Sarah told me. "I knew the first time I met your mother that someone in her family was headed for serious trouble. When I realized it was Simon, I also knew that I couldn't help him completely escape the danger. He would have to face it and be saved. That's why I drew the shield around you, so you could help him. And that's what you have to do now."

"Oh, brother," I said. "I know all about the liquor and the dance. And believe me, I'm pretty upset about it, too. This is not the first time he's done something awful like this. But I have no idea how I can help him. If I can't tell my parents, can I tell Carrie? I

62

can't tell any teachers. I don't know what to do."

"You are such a dear girl," Sarah said. "I know how hard this is for you. But don't worry. I'll work out all the details. I just need you to help me keep an eye on Simon until the danger passes completely. He's a very unique person, your brother, and despite his problems, he has some extraordinary powers. But you are pretty exceptional yourself."

I smiled, despite the fluttering in my stomach I felt whenever she mentioned Simon and danger. I was glad that Jeremiah was beside me, hearing how exceptional and dear I was. In this weirdest of all houses, I was now feeling strong, brave, smart, attractive, thin, and athletic. I had no idea who this new person I had turned into was, but I was certain Sarah was responsible for her creation. I didn't care what she did, as long as she let me remain that way a little longer. I wasn't stupid. I knew my new gifts had to come at a cost. Whatever the price, however, I was willing to pay. "Whatever you want me to do to help Simon," I told Sarah, "I will be delighted to do. Just give me a better protection shield and my instructions and I'm all yours."

seven
D

For the next hour, I sat on the love seat beside Jeremiah while Sarah gave me a quick class on spells. Well, she called it a discussion of herbal remedies to some of life's problems, but to me it seemed like good old-fashioned magic. It was fun to listen to her explain exactly how each potion worked, but it was a lot more fun to look at Jeremiah and study the contours of his face, the fit of his jeans, and the thick shiny hair on his head.

"These are some essential tools with which I want you to arm yourself so that you can be of the most aid to your brother," Sarah explained to me, while I noted that Jeremiah's fingernails were short and neat. I'd never noticed a guy's fingernails before. "I wish I could explain everything to you, but I can't always understand it all myself. I do know that your brother is not an ordinary person and that we must resort to powerful methods to reach and help him. Not only will Simon's weaknesses be strengthened by your aid, but also, as a bonus, you will derive extra strength from these assets."

"Amazing," I said. "I can hardly wait to get all this stuff." I ran my hands through the pockets of my delightfully loose jeans. The pockets were empty, but my hands smelled funny when I took them out.

Sarah smiled warmly. I forced myself to concentrate on her words as she continued to hand me weird-smelling canvas bundles, all tied with a different color string and clearly marked with a small tag. Some were small, the size of a sandwich bag, while others were much larger, at least as big as a shopping bag.

"Here is some feverfew to protect Simon—and you also, of course—against sickness and accidents, and some basil to ward off evil," Sarah explained patiently. "I also included some broom tops for you to put in water for aspurging and a lot of garlic to keep evil away. I gathered some vervain for you both with my left hand at the rise of the Dog Star, Sirius. And I also added some High John the Conqueror root, laurel, mandrake, motherwort, and patchouli. They will all help you help Simon. Some you can sprinkle in his car or bed or on his clothes, or even in the shower. I've written notes on each bag.

"Your brother's very confused about what he's doing, but each one of these offerings will point him in a safe direction. There is a potency in my necklace which I have used on every bag I am giving you. My pentacle contains my greatest powers, and I have touched each bag with this special necklace. I believe in Simon's innate strength and goodness. I will do everything I can to make those decent qualities succeed."

I thought I felt a flinch at my side as Jeremiah appeared to stiffen noticeably. I glanced at him. The smile on his face faded a bit. I smiled at him and he smiled back. Not a great warm smile but still a smile. I just hoped that the new and varied smells now surrounding me weren't offending him. He must be pretty used to this stuff. Suddenly, all I felt was tired. Wicked tired. "Wow, am I feeling out of it." I sighed. When Jeremiah wrapped his arm around my shoulders, I fell back against it.

"Of course, you are," Jeremiah said sympathetically. "My mother has powers so strong none of us can comprehend what she's doing. But so long as we believe in her, she can continue doing her vital work. Saving the lives of cardiac patients, finding lost children, keeping teenagers free from danger."

I looked directly into Jeremiah's eyes. They were, of course, black, but they possessed a warmth and gentleness that made it impossible for me to tear my own eyes away from them. I'd had crushes on guys before, but nothing like this. Everything about Jeremiah's face and body made me weak with desire. "Do you two think you could explain to me exactly how I'm going to get Simon away from all the alcohol I'm sure he bought for the dance?" I asked. "I mean, my mother's going to want to know a lot more than that I strengthened him with some garlic."

Sarah and Jeremiah looked at each other. "I didn't want to have to go into all this," Sarah said finally. "But you and your mother certainly have a right to know more than you do. If Simon goes to the dance with all the alcohol he bought last night, he's going to get into very serious trouble. Someone who drinks the alcohol could become deathly ill, and Simon will be responsible. We are dealing with a matter of life and death here. It's no longer a little joke, Emily."

"Oh, wow," I moaned, still feeling drowsy but forcing myself to stay alert. "Can't you just figure out where he put the alcohol and take it away from him?" I asked. "I could check around the house. There are only a few places he could hide it."

"It's not that simple," Sarah said. "Your brother is a determined young man. This time he's stepped over the line of mischief to serious crime. You have to trust me and let me take care of this in my own way."

"My mother's going to get ballistic when she hears all this," I said. "My dad, too. I think Simon might be on some kind of probation, and another scene with alcohol could do him in."

"It's so unfair, isn't it?" Jeremiah said, looking at me with genuine sadness. "Simon makes his messes and you have to clean them up. I know it's hard on your parents, but they're the ones with the responsibility. You're just the kid sister. Why should it be so hard on you?"

"Because Emily is an exceptional young woman," Sarah answered for me. "She has a sensitivity beyond her years. And I intend to make sure that her life is a lot easier from now on. I'm going to change Simon. I know you have trouble believing that, Emily, but it's true. Just have some faith in me and it will happen."

"You mean with a little garlic and rosemary, I'll have a normal brother?" I asked. "Someone who will not turn our house into an insane asylum every time he walks through the door?" I don't know what got into me, but tears started streaming down my face. "Because the way we're all living now stinks. I hate it so much. My parents never stay happy for more than a day or so. And even when things are good, you can still feel the tension. It's like we're all waiting for the next bomb to blow us away. You know what I wish?" Both Sarah and Jeremiah nodded. "I wish Simon would get caught by the police before the dance even starts and be thrown into jail and stay there and let the three of us have a decent life until I go off to college. One of these days, my mom or dad is just going to have a heart attack because of something my brother has done.''

I stopped talking, but I kept crying. Jeremiah wrapped both his arms around me and held me. Actually, the second his arms went around me, I stopped crying.

It was after seven o'clock when I finally emerged from Sarah's house, and I wasn't the least bit tired. Even though she had been waiting for me for over two hours, my mother was surprisingly calm. "Weren't you worried about me?" I asked when I saw her sitting in the car, reading a book about the ancient Egyptians. "How come you didn't ring Sarah's bell or call the house from your car phone?"

She looked up at me, smiled, and closed her book carefully. "Of course, I was worried about you," she said. "But I have great confidence in Sarah. Unlike with any psychiatrist we've seen, I believe in this woman. I can't explain it, honey, but the minute you walked into that house, I stopped worrying about Simon. I just know he's going to be fine. And you, too, sweetheart. I know you're going to be fine, too."

"Well, I am fine," I admitted. "Sarah gave me some stuff to give to Simon, or at least to sprinkle in his bed or clothes or car or shower. She really thinks she can make him normal." I was dying to tell her about my deep love for Jeremiah, but decided I'd better wait. Not that she wouldn't be happy I'd at long last found my one true love, but my mother needed to have her son fixed up before she could concentrate on my love life. "She did some sort of a spell, and I guess she figured out what Simon's latest problem was and she's hard at work fixing it. She says when she's finished with him, he's going to be a great kid."

"Sure sounds weird, doesn't it?" My mother sighed as she pulled her car out of Sarah's yard. "I have to be honest with you, Emily. When I hear about spells and sprinkling things on Simon's clothes, I start to get a little scared that I'm actually trusting a witch. Maybe I'm letting this whole thing go too far, letting Sarah Goody make me feel there's hope for my screwed-up son. Maybe we just shouldn't see her again and I should start acting like Simon's mother."

I don't know what came over me, because I have never acted this way before in my life, but I grabbed my mother's right arm away from the steering wheel with such force she nearly plowed into a tree. She put her foot on the brake, and we came to a screeching stop at the end of Sarah's driveway. "You can't do that," I said with far more force than I intended. "If you do, you'll jeopardize Simon's safety. We've gone this far with Sarah. We have to go all the way. No one else has ever made us feel like there's hope. Let's trust her, Mom. Please."

My mother stared at me as if I were a crazy person, which I guess I was. She reached across the seat and touched my hair, then my nose, my lips, and my neck. When she was satisfied I was still Emily, she sat up straight in her seat. "I guess I'm really too worn out to fight," she said wearily. "Besides, just this second, I got another amazing insight that Simon is going to turn out just great. It's the same thing I was feeling the whole time you were inside Sarah's house. Let's face it. Sarah can't be any crazier than me. And I'm starved. Dad has a meeting and I didn't make any supper. Let's go get some huge sandwiches at the deli." She stopped talking for a second and sniffed the air around her. "There is the weirdest smell in this car, isn't there?'' I nodded. "Sort of like garlic," she added. I nodded again. "Oh, well, I bet the corned beef and chopped liver kills that smell."

"Take me to the corned beef," I ordered, and watched in amazement as she calmly pulled her car away from the tree and drove us to Goldbuck's Deli. Never had I been more starved. I ran my hands through my pockets of my jeans again. They were still loose. And my hands smelled weirder than before. But the wart was completely gone. Sarah had told me it would take two weeks for the wart to disappear and it was gone already. At the rate this woman worked, maybe it would take only two days to make my brother normal.

eight
&

O*ur dinner at the deli did not turn out to be quite as much* fun as we had both anticipated. We called Simon from the deli to see if he wanted to join us or wanted us to bring him a sandwich, but he wasn't home. "I'm sure he'll be back any minute," my mom told me when she returned from the phone booth. "I feel so much better knowing Sarah is helping us straighten things out."

"Absolutely," I agreed as I grabbed a pickle out of the bowl in the center of our table. "He's probably on his way home right now."

My mom called the house at least two more times while we were eating, but no one answered the phone. "He promised me he would be home by seven o'clock," my mother reminded me twice during dinner. "Where do you think he is?" I felt like calling Sarah and asking her to join us and answer my mother's questions, but instead I sat and tried in vain to enjoy my corned beef sandwich.

When we arrived home and found no trace of Simon, my mother was ready to cry. She went right to the phone and called Sarah, and they spoke for at least ten minutes. Or, I should say, Sarah spoke for about ten minutes. All my mother said was "I have no idea where Simon is." When she hung up the phone, my mom was noticeably happier. "Come, honey," she ordered me. "We're sprinkling those herbs you have on Simon's bed and clothes, and then we're going to try to follow Sarah's directions on levitation. She's certain that will help me calm down."

Sarah had given my mom a pretty simple explanation of how to get one's body off the floor and into the air. Or at least it had *seemed* simple. All we had to do was lie perfectly still, our arms held in tightly by our sides and our eyes closed, and mentally propel our bodies upward. We each held a stick of blue chalk, so we could mark the spot on the wall that we passed on our way up to the ceiling. We'd also lit some incense and sprinkled our heads with a potion my mom made of springwater, some yellowish plant called frankincense, and a pinch of wolf's hair. I think Sarah gave her those last two items, but I did get it out of Mom that the wolf's hair came from a live, shedding wolf. As soon as I heard that, I stopped asking questions and quietly followed directions.

After nearly two hours on the living room rug, neither of us had made much headway. Early in our session, my mother had thought she was floating, but by the time I opened my eyes she was back on the floor. "It was unbelievable!" she gushed excitedly. "I have never felt freer in my whole life. Like I was a feather headed up to the sky. A dove soaring through the clouds. Oh, God, it's awful to be stuck back on this miserable floor."

Unfortunately, neither Mom nor I did make it back up there. But we were so intent that we never heard my father walk into the house. He was a bit overwhelmed when he saw the two of us lying on the floor, our eyes tightly closed. "What the hell is going on here?" he shouted, scaring my mom so badly she screamed.

I was a little more controlled. I bolted upright into a sitting position, more frustrated by the fact that I hadn't left the beige rug than my father's annoying presence. "Geez, Dad," I asked, "do you have to shout like that? You really frightened me and Mom."

"Oh, I did, huh?" he said real sarcastically. "Well, you'll just have to forgive me for behaving so rudely. You see, I got a little concerned when I came in and found my wife and daughter lying on the floor like they'd been tied up and executed. I guess the fact that my son who disappeared for most of last night doesn't appear to be home tonight also has me a bit uptight. You know, maybe I'm just more suspicious about two bodies on the floor than I might normally be. But it sure would help my fragile state of mind if one of you could please tell me what is going on around here. And what the devil is that weird smell? And why are your heads damp? It smells like a zoo in here."

There was no doubt my dad was upset. And getting angrier by the second. My mother was no help. After she screamed, she just glanced at my father, closed her eyes, and went back to her levitation attempts. It was unbelievable. I honestly believe she thought she could just levitate herself right out of the room, out of the house, and out of our lives. "Hey, Mom," I suggested. "Let's can this for a while, okay? Maybe we can take off later tonight."

"Take off where?" my father asked. "What are you talking about, Emily?"

"We were practicing our levitation abilities," I told him. It just seemed easier to give him some truth. I felt awful not telling him what Sarah had told me

73

about Simon and the alcohol he'd bought in New Hampshire. "Sarah Goody told us about levitation and it seemed like fun." The look on his face was somewhere between fury and horror, with a little pity and a lot of fear for our sanity thrown in. Plus, his nose was all wrinkled up. He was right. The room did smell like a zoo.

"Look, Dad," I continued, trying not to look into his eyes, "it's all part of Mom's story. She thought it might be interesting to add something about her attempt to levitate. You know, just to give the story some real authority. Plus, it would make a good picture to go with the story, don't you think? Mom floating around near the ceiling. I swear, we could be talking Pulitzer Prize here."

"We're talking insanity here," he said, but he did seem calmer. My mother was still on the carpet with her eyes closed and her arms at her sides. She looked incredibly peaceful. My dad focused his attention on me. "But I really don't care whether you two are on the floor or the ceiling. I'd just like some information on Simon. When exactly is he coming home, and where was he last night?"

"Oh, Simon," I said, and took a deep breath. Usually, I'm the world's worst liar. Whenever I try to lie my way out of a bad situation, I stutter and contradict myself, making it a thousand times worse. Simon, on the other hand, is the world's best liar. Sometimes he can tell me a story that I know for a fact is untrue, but by the time I finish listening to him, I've convinced myself I was dead wrong and he is telling the absolute truth. I swear, my brother could convince a dead person he was alive.

"Simon's fine," I began, forcing myself to look my father right in the eye, something I never do when

I'm lying. "He called to say he was working on a history paper with Mike. He says he was at the Boston College library last night working on the same paper. Mom thinks he was lying. That's probably why she's just lying there like that now. Simon said he wasn't sure when he was coming home."

"Oh, Emmy," he said, shaking his head sadly. All the anger had disappeared from his voice. "I don't know how much more any of us can take. It probably would be great if he stayed away a month. Well, at least we know he's safe inside a twenty-four-hour library. Not that I believe for one second that he's studying there. He's probably sleeping off a booze scene. Forgive me, honey, but I'm too wiped out to stay up. I barely slept last night. I'm going to bed now." He glanced at my mother. She looked sound asleep. "I hate to disturb her. She's had a rougher time than I have. I'll get a blanket and pillow for her. 'Night, honey."

" 'Night, Daddy," I said, and gave him a hug.

When he kissed the top of my head, he choked for a second and then pulled some brown hairs out of his mouth. "Did you get a haircut today?" he asked me just before he left the living room.

"Yeah," I lied again, certain my poor father had just gotten a mouthful of wolf's hair. Part of me felt terrible for deceiving him, but another part felt wonderful. My exhausted father was going to get some well-deserved rest—thanks to his daughter, who had suddenly turned into a master liar. I did have a moment of panic that my brother might really be in danger but it was fleeting. My brother was at Mike Richmond's doing anything besides working on a school paper, or back in New Hampshire buying more alcohol for next Friday's school dance, or maybe

Sarah had found him and taken him to her house, where he was now surrounded by wet broom tops and herbs, getting fixed up. No matter where he was, he wasn't home.

After my father went to bed, I stayed in the living room with my mother for a while, trying desperately to levitate. A couple of times, I thought I had it, but the feeling of weightlessness never lasted more than a few seconds. But, man, did it feel good. So good that it was hard to stop trying to get it back. It must have been around two in the morning when I finally decided I'd had enough. All I was doing by then was nodding off to sleep and dreaming I was floating around the light fixture on the ceiling. My mother also looked like she was sleeping, so I got up and went over to the doorway to get the pillow and blanket my dad had brought down for her. When I turned around, my mother was halfway between the floor and the ceiling. I watched, stunned, while she floated toward the ceiling, her body stiff and unmoving. I was so jealous I wanted to cry. But I didn't do that. Instead, I stood there, my mouth open, certain that any second my mother was going to levitate right through the ceiling and head so far up into the sky that she would never come back.

But that didn't happen. While I watched, horrified, my mother fell back to the ground, landing on the rug with a terrible thud. Her body shook painfully for a few seconds and then was perfectly still. I raced to her side and sank to my knees beside her. Her eyes were still closed, she was clutching the piece of blue chalk, and she had the weirdest expression on her face. For one hideous second, I thought she was dead. But before I could scream, my mother opened her eyes, sat up, and stared at me, her face covered with a deliciously sweet, happy expression.

"Oh, Emily," she said softly, her voice no more than a whisper, "I was there. And it was beautiful."

"Where were you?" I asked. "Describe it exactly."

"I was so high up I could see the whole world below me. I was at peace with everyone and everything that was a part of my life. Nothing could hurt me up there. I was completely safe. It was heavenly."

"You have to take me there," I told her. "It's not fair that you get to go and I don't. Please tell me exactly what you did."

"Of course, darling," my mother said in a singsong voice I'd never heard before. "We'll go there together. You and I."

I was still amazed that my mother hadn't been hurt when she'd fallen from the ceiling. But this new voice of hers was even harder to digest. My mother always spoke quickly and nervously. That was as much a part of her as her long, black, curly hair. The woman who'd tumbled away from the ceiling talked slowly and gently. But I ignored her weird voice and plowed ahead. "Come on, Mom. Show me how to do it. Now."

"Of course, darling," she told me again. "Just lie back and close your eyes and imagine the clouds above your head. Beautiful white fluffy clouds that are beckoning to you to come join them. And birds. Imagine dozens of white doves that are calling your name and swooping down to you. Let the doves carry you up to the clouds. Leave your pain and troubles here, and allow the joy of life to fill your body with the power to lift you. It's so easy if you just do that."

I lay beside her, clutching my piece of blue chalk,

and tried to imagine doves and clouds. But all I could think about was how strange my mother sounded. For another hour, I tried to release the pain and let the joy kick in, but the only thing that kicked in was overwhelming fatigue. I have no idea if my mother made it to the ceiling again, but I didn't. I fell asleep, and when I awoke, my mother was gone. I checked the ceiling, but she was nowhere to be seen. All I noticed was a blue chalk mark on the bottom of the light fixture ten feet above me. I looked at my watch and saw that it was nearly five o'clock. It wasn't easy, but I dragged myself off the beige rug and staggered upstairs to my bedroom.

Before I went into my room, I glanced inside my parents' bedroom. My father was alone in their king-size bed. Quickly, I checked out Simon's room. Unbelievable. He was back in his bed again. And the room sure smelled funny. Not from the alcohol which I was sure he'd consumed, but rather from the sprinkling my mother and I had performed. It was amazing he could sleep so peacefully with all those smells. I looked upward and didn't see my mother floating around near his ceiling. I was going to go downstairs and see if she was in the kitchen, but I was so exhausted I had to go into my own room and lie down for a second.

As soon as I flopped down on my bed and closed my eyes, I saw my mother floating around the ceiling of the Halloween-decorated school gym. Man, did her face look untroubled. "I'm coming," I told her. "I'll be there in a flash." But my body stayed on top of my pink-and-white-striped comforter. I tried to move it into the gym, but it wouldn't move one speck upward. I was going to get under my comforter, but I held my hands tightly to my sides and thought about the doves for just a minute. The next thing I knew I was banging my head on the light fixture above my bed. I was only up there a few seconds, but it was enough. I was hooked. I'd seen the view; I'd found my wings; and I was out of there.

nine
D

I *was so groggy the next morning that I could barely*
muster the strength to get dressed. I knew I could have
convinced my mother to let me stay home, but I had
to go to school, if for no other reason than to keep an
eye on my brother, who had amazed me by getting
out the door, in a surprising good mood, before me.
Our mother never saw us when we left, and the living
room wall had at least two new blue chalk marks. No
wonder the poor woman was sleeping. She'd spent the
entire night flying around our house. She must have
been exhausted . . . and frustrated that she'd ended up
back down here again.

My father's hardware store was beginning its an-
nual Halloween sale on lawn mowers, which sounds
ridiculous since the store is in New England and there
isn't a blade of grass showing anywhere at that time.
Strangely enough, it's a big moneymaker. My father
puts a lot of time and energy into the sale and says
it's a big factor in keeping his store successful. All I
know is that it always causes a big fight. Every year,
my father would ask Simon to help out during the
first hectic week of the sale, and every year, Simon
would refuse. "You're a big, strong kid," my father

would remind Simon. "Is it asking too much for you to come down to the store a few days after school and for one lousy weekend to help me drag lawn mowers out to customers' cars?"

"Yup," Simon always answered him. "It kills my back."

And then they'd argue about Simon's back, which never hurt except during the sale. And my mother would get into it and aggravate both of them. She'd tell my father he shouldn't lay a guilt trip on his son, and then she'd lay a guilt trip on Simon. It always got ugly, and I got stomach pains every time I saw a lawn mower. It didn't seem to matter that I helped out all I could during the sale. I was pretty good at the cash register, but I couldn't carry lawn mowers to customers' cars.

"Think I have any chance of getting your brother over to the store today?" my father asked me as I was putting my books into my backpack. "Maybe if I turn it into a liquor store, huh?"

I smiled weakly. "Yeah," I agreed, keeping my eye on the clock. I had less than five minutes to finish my cereal, brush my teeth, and get out the door.

"It's unbelievable," Dad said, getting angrier with each word. "I'm incredibly short of help this weekend. I don't know how I'm going to get through this sale without him. But I know there's not one chance in a million that he'll help me."

"He hasn't helped you in years," I reminded my father. "Why are you relying on him now?"

"I always rely on him," my father said indignantly. "Just because he disappoints me every year doesn't mean I don't rely on him. But this year, I really need him. Joe's brother always gives me a hand, but he broke his leg in a hockey game last week. God forbid your brother should just once help me out of a jam, instead of always creating one.''

I saw Carrie coming up the front walk. I had another math quiz first period. I had to get out of there immediately, but I felt terrible abandoning my father like that. "I have someone who can help you," I said, as surprised as my father by my announcement. "His name is Jeremiah. He's from Salem. I promise he'll be there sometime today." I couldn't believe myself. I had absolutely no idea if Jeremiah would help my father. Or if he knew what a lawn mower was. All I knew was that he was gorgeous and he was Sarah Goody's son. But something told me he would help my father. I gave my dad a quick peck on his cheek, grabbed my books, and ran out to meet Carrie. It killed me to leave the house without brushing my teeth, but I had no choice. I had to get to math on time. As I closed the front door behind me, I realized I no longer felt the least bit tired.

Of course, I aced my math quiz, shocking poor Ms. Madorsky a second time. During lunch, I ran to the phone booth and called Sarah Goody. She wasn't there, but I left a message on her machine asking Jeremiah if he was free that afternoon to help my father sell lawn mowers. I knew it was a strange message, but I couldn't see any reason to beat around the bush. As soon as I finished my call, I ran into Brian Walsh, who looked as if he had been waiting for me to come out of the booth. "How you doing?" he asked me.

"Fine," I said. Man, did he look cute, different from the other love of my life, Jeremiah, the gorgeous, witchy guy, but still awfully cute. Brian was wearing jeans and a maroon Boston College sweatshirt, and his longish sand-colored hair was covering part of his green eyes. He was a real jock, with an incredible way of looking hunky and cute at the same time. I couldn't figure out how he did it. All I knew was that he did it—and did something to me as well. I'd been adoring him from a distance for months, but this was the first time the two of us ever had a real conversation.

"You look great," he told me, and I began to wonder if this was all a bad joke. Maybe someone had put him up to this. Maybe someone had bet him a hundred dollars that he couldn't go up to ugly old Emily Silver and tell her she looked great.

"Thanks," I said, waiting for a bunch of his friends to race into sight and drop dead laughing on the ground behind him.

But they didn't show up. And he kept on talking to me. "Want to go to the Halloween dance next Friday night?" he asked as normally as if he were asking Carrie. Which I suddenly remembered Carrie thought he might do. I'd never had the nerve to tell Carrie I had a serious crush on one of her many boyfriends for the past six months. Besides, it wouldn't have mattered. None of the guys who liked her would ever have been interested in me. But things were different now. Still, there was no way I could hurt my best friend by going to the dance with someone she liked.

Suddenly, I remembered Simon, and for the first time in my life, thinking of my brother provided me some pleasure. Carrie really liked Simon. She'd far rather go to the dance with him than with Brian. Somehow, I'd figure out a way to make certain she went with Simon. My problems were over; all I needed to do was to say "Sure," but I couldn't get the word out. So, I nodded.

And I guess that was enough, because then Brian

said, "Great. I'll call you. See ya." And he was gone.

When I found Jeremiah standing by my locker after my last class ended, I didn't faint or anything like that. I just smiled casually, as if it were the most normal thing in the world for a tall, handsome, dark guy dressed in black jeans, a black T-shirt, and black boots to be standing there, waiting for me. Nothing in my life was normal anymore. I wasn't normal anymore. I had a mad crush on Brian. Brian had invited me to the dance. I thought Jeremiah was absolutely gorgeous. Jeremiah had come to my school to see me. I quickly glanced at my locker, remembered the combination, and the door immediately swung open without my touching the lock. Yup, this was my life now. "Hi, Jeremiah," I said, smiling broadly. "What's up?"

"I thought I'd drive you over to the hardware store," he said.

"Great idea," I said, noticing that Jeremiah's eyes were so black they gave *black* a new meaning. *Black* now meant shimmering and sexy and luminous and powerful and red-hot. Brian Walsh might have been cute, but this figure standing in front of my locker was sumptuous. Swallowing a deep, searing hunger, I put away my math and Spanish books and took out my English and history books, every movement a study in grace and serenity. When I suddenly remembered my overdue library book, it appeared on top of my history book. No big deal.

"Hey, there." Carrie's voice was like a shrill whistle in my ear as she approached my locker. "I'm off to fight the drinking war," she said excitedly. "You won't believe it but I just convinced Arlene Peterson to work with me on a joint proposal. She's rounding up everybody she can for an emergency meeting of the student council. We're going to present it to them. Oh, God, I hope this one works. Wish me luck.''

I couldn't believe it. I'd totally forgotten Carrie. She'd told me about her plan to work with Arlene during our walk to school. This was her last chance to get any sort of an antidrinking proposal passed. I'd never seen her work so hard for anything. Failure was not something Carrie accepted, but this project was going very poorly for her. Still, if anyone was going to succeed against long odds, my buddy was the one. She looked adorable in her navy corduroy overalls and red-and-white-checkered work shirt. But she was going to have to do a lot more than look terrific. Especially with the alcohol problems my brother, whom I selfishly hoped would be her date, was going to create next Friday night. Jeremiah was a god sent from the heavens, but Carrie was my best friend on earth. And I wished with all my heart that her wish would come true. I hugged her tightly. ''Go get 'em, Carrie,'' I told her. ''Just remember to stress the positive. And keep things going with Arlene. She's your ticket to success.''

''And make Ellen Waring, not Arlene Peterson, your co-chairman,'' Jeremiah added.

Carrie and I both jumped at the sound of his voice. Of course, I knew he was there. But Carrie, I suddenly realized, hadn't seen him. How was that possible? The guy was over six feet tall. And his shoulders were broad and imposing. Was he invisible? Was I in love with a ghost who was also a witch's son? ''Hi, there,'' Carrie said, smiling sweetly. Obviously, he wasn't a ghost. ''Now, who's this?''

''I'm Jeremiah Brooks,'' Jeremiah said, reaching

out to shake her hand. "A good friend of Emily's. I presume you're Carrie."

"Sure am," she said, her eyes locked on the black eyes for which I would gladly have traded both of my thumbs. And a couple of my teeth. "It's nice to meet you. But how do you know Ellen Waring?"

"I know that her father and her older brother Danny have both had a tough time with drinking, and that she's desperate to do something. She's a very strong-minded young woman. If you can get her on your side, your project will succeed."

"You're incredible," Carrie said, and I began to get nervous that she meant for reasons other than his suggestion for saving her beloved project from failure. "How on earth do you know all these things? And how can I ever thank you for sharing them with me?" I couldn't believe the way Carrie was looking at Jeremiah. She was flirting. Batting her eyelashes in a shameless way. Looking even more adorable than when she'd walked over to my locker. I stood there, horrified, while the sexiest, blackest eyes in the world stared back at my former best friend.

"The Warings are friends of my family," he answered. "My mother's known Mrs. Waring for years. She once told me Ellen's on the student council. As soon as you mentioned a drinking war, her name popped into my mind. Just speak to her before the meeting."

Carrie looked at her watch. "Oh, God, the meeting starts in five minutes. I'd better race over there and catch her. Thank you so so so much. Wish me luck, Emmy."

"Good luck," I said, and she was gone. I saw the way Jeremiah's eyes followed her down the corridor, and I felt sick to my stomach. And then I remembered

Brian Walsh and I felt even sicker. What was going on? The guy I'd been crazy about for months but who had always been crazy about my best friend had just asked me to the dance and I had accepted. But now I was getting crazy about a guy I'd just met whose mother was a witch, and it was making me crazy that my best friend just might be getting a tiny bit crazy about him, too. It was simple. I was crazy. Certifiable.

I was contemplating walking into my locker and sealing the door behind me when a familiar voice said "Hi, there." I looked up and saw Brian Walsh and three of his soccer teammates. "What's up?"

"Oh, hi, Brian," I said in that cool, graceful manner that seemed to come over me now whenever gorgeous guys approached me. "Nothing much." I saw Brian look at Jeremiah, and I saw Jeremiah look at Brian, and it didn't take witchcraft to read their silent reaction. It wasn't love at first sight. Brian seemed confused by Jeremiah's presence, and Jeremiah seemed amused by Brian's. For one wonderful, awful second I thought they might come to blows, but instead they both looked at me. "Brian, this is my friend Jeremiah from Salem," I said. "Jeremiah, this is Brian, my friend from school." Not a particularly brilliant introduction, but the best I could do. I had to do better. "Jeremiah is here to help my father with his lawn mower sale. We're going over to the store right now."

But no one looked like he was heading anywhere. Jeremiah stood perfectly still, staring at Brian, who was standing perfectly still while his three soccer buddies were coming closer to me and Jeremiah. And then it happened. Jeremiah smiled. And Brian smiled. And all six of us walked out of the school together, me at the front, flanked by Jeremiah and Brian and trailed by the three soccer buddies, who, like Brian, were all in their soccer shorts and shirts, headed for a game, or at least a practice, which they had decided to ignore so they could go to a lawn mower sale. If this was all due to a protection spell, I liked it.

I saw heads turn as we moved through the corridor, out the front door, and down the stairs to the parking lot. Ordinary, chubby Emily Silver, surrounded by five hunky guys, sliding into the front seat of a black BMW. Obviously, removing warts earned big bucks for witches. The four soccer stars climbed into the roomy back seat, seemingly unbothered by their decision to cut their game or practice. The black car pulled gracefully away from the curb. It was a sight not to be believed.

Surprised would not, however, be a good word to describe my father's reaction when the six of us walked into his hardware store. "Need some help with those lawn mowers, Mr. Silver?" Jeremiah asked my dad.

"Sure," he answered, shaking his head as the guys began unloading lawn mowers from the truck parked outside the store, moving each one as easily as if it were a plastic toy. I took my place behind the cash register and watched silently as my father began barking orders to his five new assistants.

For as far back as I could remember, the lawn mower sale had been a scene of fighting and frustration for my family. That day, it was a scene from the *Happy Lawn Mower Sale* movie. When the first customer handed me her slip, I cheerfully rang up her sale and handed her the receipt. I watched as Jeremiah picked up her bright green lawn mower and carried it to her car. He winked at me as he walked out the door. I was about to fall in a delirious swoon when

Brian approached my register. "Neat store, Emily," he told me.

"Thanks," I said.

"Don't forget Friday night," he reminded me as he walked over to give a customer a hand.

"I won't," I said as Jeremiah walked back into the store. For a brief second I saw something flash across the blackest eyes in the world. I understood it immediately. It was exactly what I'd felt when I'd seen Carrie flirt with Jeremiah. It was jealousy, beautiful unabated jealousy. But it was a different kind of jealousy than what I'd experienced earlier that afternoon. Jeremiah's jealousy, like everything about him, was black. Only that black wasn't sensuous and amorous. It was scary. Wicked scary.

ten

I finally saw Simon next Friday evening, a few minutes before seven. I was running around like a crazy person trying to get ready for the Halloween dance when he walked into my bedroom. I had decided to go as Dorothy from *The Wizard of Oz*. Brian had told me his brother had a dog costume he could borrow, so we were going as Dorothy and Toto. I was in the midst of braiding my hair when Simon appeared. He was dressed like a bum, with ragged jeans; a tattered, dirty, white, Grateful Dead T-shirt; and crummy, ripped sneakers. His hair was uncombed and sticking out all over his head, and he was unshaven and looking exceptionally gross. Since Simon always, even in his most repulsive states, looked handsome and perfectly groomed, this was quite a costume.

"Great getup," I said, glad finally to see him. I'd been looking for him for a couple of days and hadn't run into him in school or after classes. He'd spent very little time at home, avoiding my father and his lawn mowers, I was certain. I had, however, been sprinkling the contents of two of Sarah's bags on his bed and his clothes and had snuck a couple of pictures of Carrie into his bureau and backpack. Carrie still didn't have a date for the dance, and even though she insisted she had no problem going without a date, or my going with Brian, I felt bad. It made me feel better that she was pumped over the fact that the student council had been much more enthusiastic over her antidrinking plan and was arranging for a meeting with teachers and parents to take place in a few weeks. "I could barely recognize you," I told my brother as I picked up a photograph of Carrie from my desk.

"What getup?" he asked, ignoring the photograph but started rummaging around the top of my desk.

"Your bum costume," I said, unhappy at the sight of his rather dirty hands moving all over the top of my desk. It wasn't a neat desk, but it was my private property. "I guarantee you no one will recognize you. Hey, is there something you're looking for?"

He stopped and looked up at me. "You don't look ugly," he told me. "That will guarantee that no one will recognize you. But I haven't put my costume on. Actually, I don't have a costume. That's what I'm looking for."

"A costume on my desk?" I asked, trying to ignore his barbs. I couldn't quite figure out if what he had just said to me was a direct insult or not. I had a strong feeling it was not flattering.

"Yeah. I figured I could find something stupid enough on your desk to qualify as a costume. And your little friend, what's her name? The cute one you hang around with all the time who makes you look even uglier?"

It was getting harder to ignore him. His latest barb was definitely an insult. "Do you mean Carrie?" I asked, feeling both nervous and excited as well as hurt. Had I actually pushed my dearest friend into this awful person's arms?

"Yeah, Carrie," he said. "I don't know her last name, so give me her number. I need to call her."

"She's probably left for the dance," I told him, regretting everything I'd done to bring the two of them together. I couldn't do this to Carrie. I'd give her Brian. I'd stay home.

Simon looked at me hard. "Just give me her lousy number," he said. "Not her schedule."

"Why?" I asked. I saw my brother getting angry, but I didn't care. He couldn't hurt me any more than he already had.

" 'Cause I'm taking her to the dance, okay? Are you her mother or something? Do I have to get your permission?"

I couldn't believe what I was hearing. It was over. I'd ruined Carrie's life. "When did you ask Carrie to the dance?" I asked.

Simon took his hands off my desk. I could see that I actually had some power over him. He wanted that number. Bad. "I ran into her in the hall after my last class. That's all I'm telling you. Now, give me the miserable number or your little buddy's going to be standing outside her house all night waiting for me to pick her up."

None of this made any sense to me. But I hadn't seen Carrie after school. She'd had a student council meeting, and I'd gone back to my father's store to help out with his sale. After I got home, I'd been so busy with my costume I hadn't called her. But there was no way she would have made a date with Simon and not called me. No way. My God, what had I done? I told my brother her number and watched silently as he muttered the number to himself and left my room.

It wasn't easy, but I waited ten minutes, and then

I dialed the number myself. Carrie answered on the first ring. "What is going on with you and my brother?" I asked the minute I heard her voice. "You two have a date and you didn't say a word to me?" I hated the way I sounded, like a cranky old lady, but it was just too unbelievable that such a thing had happened in the first place, never mind that I'd caused it to happen and she hadn't told me it had.

"After I met Simon, I ran to the phone booth outside the gymnasium and called you at the hardware store," she said, her voice nervous and excited. "Your father took the number and promised you'd call me right back, but you didn't. I told him it was urgent. I waited and waited, and you didn't call, and I didn't have another cent on me. Then Mrs. Kramer came out and said she had to use the phone. So I went inside to help with the decorations. I just got home a few minutes ago, and Simon called the second I walked in. I asked him if you were home, but he said you already left. Where are you anyhow? And why didn't you call me from the hardware store?"

"Because my idiot father never gave me the message," I said. "And my brother's a liar, in case you didn't already know that. Just tell me what happened already."

"I'm still trying to figure it out myself," she said. "All I can tell you is I was walking out of French class, and there was Simon standing outside the door. He walked right up to me, gave me this wicked smile, and asked me if I wanted to go to the dance with him. I kept looking around to see if he was talking to someone else, but I was the only one there. I knew you wouldn't be happy about my going out with your brother, but the truth is, I really don't want to go to the dance stag, and you're going with Brian, which is certainly okay with me, since we weren't going out or anything, and Simon looked so cute I couldn't help it. So I said yes, and he said he'd call me around seven and that was that. Oh, Emily, I can't believe I'm going out with Simon. I know what you're thinking, but he's not as bad as you think. I've got to run now. He's going to be here any minute and I'm not in my tutu yet. Promise me you'll try and understand.''

"I'll try," I promised. Before I could say another word, she was gone and I was holding a dead telephone in one hand and a lopsided braid in the other. I was afraid to think about exactly what had happened and why. Maybe it was all pure coincidence. Maybe Carrie would turn my brother into a decent human being. Maybe my brother would pour all the alcohol he'd bought in New Hampshire down the drain. Maybe I could have one thought which had an iota of truth in it. There was nothing I could do about all the problems around me, so I hung up the phone, sat on my bed, and rebraided my hair. Then I put on the red-and-white pinafore dress my mother had borrowed from one of her friends' daughters, and carefully placed a pink lipstick, a comb, and some breath mints in the basket pocketbook my mother had also borrowed. I was all dressed and ready for the dance. I walked into Simon's room and saw that it was empty.

I bumped into my mother as I was coming out of Simon's room. She was dressed, for a change, in black. This time, she was wearing a really full black dress, black stockings, black shoes, and a huge, silver, five-sided necklace around her neck. I recognized it immediately. It was exactly like the one Sarah Goody always wore.

"What were you doing in Simon's room?" she asked me.

"Looking for a history book I can't find anywhere," I answered her, amazed at how easily I lied now. "I thought maybe Simon had hidden it or something."

My mother's face turned so sad I nearly told her the truth, but she spoke too quickly for me to get in another word. "He just left," she told me. "He looked awful, but he told me it was his costume. He said he had a date for the dance and he was in a big rush to go get her. I just know he's going to get into trouble."

I had to make the poor woman feel better "You won't believe who he's taking to the dance," I said.

She shrugged. "Barby Gold, I imagine," she said.

"No way," I said. "I already told you, she's history. He's taking Carrie."

My mother looked duly shocked, but there was a definite glimmer of pleasure on her face. "Wow," she said. "Maybe that's what Sarah was talking about."

"Sarah knew he was taking Carrie to the dance?" I asked.

"I don't know," she told me, fingering her five-sided necklace. "She just assured me he was safe and things were going to work out just fine. She said she would make sure he was in the best possible protective custody till the danger passed. I guess Carrie's the best protection anyone could ask for, don't you agree? Oh, who knows what's good or bad for him?" She brightened visibly. "Maybe this is the start of a whole new life for Simon. Heaven knows Barby Gold wasn't good for him. But Carrie—"

"What's the purpose of that necklace?" I asked, interrupting her. I'd heard the story of Simon's new life many times before. I wasn't anxious to hear it again.

"Oh, it's a pentacle," she told me. "Sarah gave it to me. It's one of the oldest geometric symbols in the world. It's the prime symbol of witchcraft, a five-pointed star with one point up, set within the circle of the full moon. The five sides stand for the five senses. Sarah charged it with special energy to help me get through this difficult time. You know, I think she's right. I do feel better with it on."

I looked at her carefully. She didn't look any better to me. If anything, she looked more tired and confused. But what did I know? She was dressed in black like an old lady and I was dressed in a pinafore like a little girl. "It's neat," I told her.

"So, are you all ready for the dance?" she asked, sounding more like my mother.

"Yeah," I answered. "Do you like my outfit?" I never had to ask my mother if she liked my clothes. She always had a suggestion on how I could look better.

"Looks great," she said. "When's Brian coming to get you?"

My mother was trying to appear interested in my plans, and she'd worked hard to get my costume together, but she was so distracted over Simon that I was amazed she'd remembered who I was going with. She knew this was my first real date, and it was a big deal to both of us. But her new worry over the unexplained danger to Simon had changed her. Part of me wanted to cry that my mother didn't care with all her heart and soul about what was happening to me, and another part didn't feel all that bad. It wasn't so terrible to have some privacy in my life.

My best friend hadn't been much more enthusiastic

over my first date than my mother. But I couldn't blame Carrie. Since we'd met in the second grade, she'd assumed the role of cheerleader in our relationship. She was always building me up and telling me how great I was. And she was always achieving something while I lagged behind. But now everything had changed. A popular boy, whom Carrie had assumed would ask her, had invited me to the Halloween dance. Simon, who, although a detestable older brother, was a highly desired date, was taking *her* to the dance. Girls would die to go out with Simon. And Carrie'd been nuts over him since we were little kids. But the truth was Brian had been her first choice, and he was my date. The position of the moon and the stars had, for the first time since second grade, shifted. And I was using every bit of energy I could muster not to fall out of the sky.

Carrie called me a short time after I walked back into my room to put the finishing touches on my costume. "Do you need me to come braid your hair?" she asked.

"What are you doing home?" I asked. "Where's Simon?"

"I'm not home, silly," she said. "I'm at school, in the phone booth outside the gym. He had to run out and get something, so I ran to call you. I have to tell you, I feel a little silly in this Tinkerbell costume. But can you believe how cute Simon looks in his derelict outfit?"

"Yeah, real cute," I lied, worried sick about where my brother had gone. It must have been to get the liquor he'd stashed somewhere, liquor which was destined to destroy the dance and Carrie's proposal and her heart, all in one fell swoop. "Look, Carrie, there's something I've got to tell you about Simon. He's—"

"Please, Emily, don't do that," she interrupted me. "I know how difficult this is for you, and I know how awful Simon can be, but have you ever thought that maybe I can help him? I know he misuses alcohol all the time and he's probably planning on drinking at the dance. But I honestly believe I can help him. I hate to sound mean, but you know your parents have tried everything to make Simon stop getting into trouble, and nothing has worked. Maybe I can do what your family couldn't. Emily, I need you to try and forget everything you know and hate about Simon, and treat him as someone I like a lot and want to have a chance to get to know. Please. Just for me, Emmy."

I'd never heard Carrie sound so desperate for my help. "I'll try," I promised, "but I still have to warn you about something very scary that Simon is planning to do tonight."

"Oh, Emily," Carrie practically hissed into the phone. "I don't believe you. You just can't let it go, can you? Well, I can. Good-bye." She was gone, and I felt like crying. But my mother's voice from outside my door was loud and clear. Brian had arrived to take me to the dance. And so I finished braiding my hair myself, muttered a silent prayer to Sarah, collected my basket pocketbook, and headed downstairs to meet my amazing date.

The dance turned out to be a blast. Maybe it was because everyone was in costume, and that made people more relaxed and less inhibited. Even though Carrie would barely look at me, I couldn't remember ever having so much fun. Guys I barely knew came up to me and asked me to dance. I did have to admit my Dorothy costume was kind of cute, but I certainly didn't look as pretty as Carrie did in her tutu. Nevertheless, every time Brian left my side for a second, some guy took my hand and led me out to the dance floor. Brian didn't look all that happy about my sudden popularity, but he made sure he was nearby when a dance ended with someone else, and we'd start dancing before anyone else approached me. I was pretty giddy from the whole experience and couldn't wipe the silly smile off my face.

Carrie, however, had no smile on her face that night. It was obvious she knew a lot of the kids were drinking, and she seemed powerless to figure out where they were getting the liquor or how to get it away from them. I meant to find a way to talk to her, but I was too busy dancing. "It's important to stop this kind of behavior," she practically barked at me during the first conversation we had all night, between sets. "It's more important than being the queen of the ball."

I might have been crushed by her last remark, but I didn't have time to process it. Before I could respond, Joel Solomon, the captain of the football team, asked me to dance. I saw the look on Carrie's face as Joel led me away. It wasn't pretty. If Tinkerbell had had a knife, Dorothy would never have made it back to Kansas. I spent the whole dance with Joel talking about Carrie, in the hope he'd seek her out for the next dance, but Joel noticed only me. I felt terrible—and useless.

Simon spent barely a second with Carrie. He was too busy running around with his idiot friends to pay any attention to her. I never saw her dance with him, but she did dance with some guy in a weird cow costume. Lots of other guys came over to her, but she shrugged them all off. Except for the cow, Simon was the only one she would dance with.

I saw Carrie talk to Ellen Waring and Arlene Peterson several times, and all three of them looked worried. The last thing they wanted before their upcoming meeting with teachers and parents was a serious alcohol problem at this dance. They needed to prove to the faculty and other student council members that the majority of students wanted to curb their drinking. If things got out of hand at this dance, the principal would simply refuse to allow the students to have any more dances or social activities.

It was a miracle that the chaperones hadn't noticed all the drinking, too. Even I saw that a large group of kids had snuck in flasks of rum and were passing them around all evening. Still, except for those kids, who I knew were not friends of Simon's, and a few others, things were still pretty much under control. It was no worse, nor any better, than the other school dances. If things didn't deteriorate, Carrie and Ellen and Arlene would probably be grateful.

At exactly ten o'clock, however, everything changed. Brian and I had just finished a wild, fast dance and had stepped into the hall outside the gym to catch our breath for a couple of minutes, when I saw Simon and his new buddy Paul Irving walk toward us. It was one of the few times I'd seen Simon all evening. He was still in his bum's costume, but there was a swagger to his walk. Paul had on a black cape and monster teeth and was carrying a huge black sack over his shoulder, but his walk was as unsteady as my brother's. The two of them were giggling and slapping each other on the back like drunken sailors. At that moment, I hated my brother so much I wanted to jump on him and pummel him until he sank unconscious to the ground. But I was in a red-and-white pinafore, holding hands with a dog. I knew the wonderful evening I was enjoying was about to come to a hideous end.

"Hey, look who's here," Simon said when he saw me. "Two dogs. Only one's wearing a weird dress."

Brian stiffened beside me. "Why don't you go home, Simon," I said, speaking as quickly as I could, wishing Paul wasn't there. If it had been just Simon and Brian, I would have put my money on Brian's brawn. "Please do us all a favor and go somewhere else. Brian and I will drive you anywhere you want to go. Okay? Just tell us where you want to go."

"We're just where we want to be," Simon said. "The perfect place for a Halloween trick or treat, right, Paul?" Paul nodded. "You could call us the treat guys. 'Cause we got a bunch of treats. Now, all of the lucky people who have already paid some good money for their treats are waiting inside for their candy, so if you'll excuse us, we're off to see the Wizard of Oz." With that, Simon practically fell to the floor laughing. It was no surprise to me that he could make such an amazing literary reference. My brother, I'd always known, was a pretty bright guy.

"Hey, just a minute," Brian said. "If you guys have some liquor stashed in that sack, you're not going into the gym. I've got no problem with your drinking, but why don't you do it outside the building with your buddies? There are plenty of kids drinking out there. Just join them, and don't ruin the night for the kids who don't want to drink."

Brian spoke so sensibly and calmly I wanted to kiss him. I knew he was on the student council with Carrie and had worked on her proposal, but I was amazed at how clearheaded and smart he sounded. I was so upset all I could do was try not to cry. But Brian was acting like an adult. His words, however, were drowned out by the insane laughter of the two idiots in front of him.

When Brian moved to take the sack from Paul's hands, the two jerks stopped laughing. "Move back, doggy boy," Simon told him, not a trace of laughter in his voice. "I've got a lot of presents for some happy trick or treaters who paid good cash for their little tricks." He opened the sack, pulled out a green plastic water pistol, and squirted Brian and me in the face. The alcohol stung my eyes and made me gasp. Brian leaped at Simon, but Paul was on him before he could land one punch. I screamed. The bum, the monster, and the dog got into one big squall, and when I saw the dog being pummeled mercilessly, I screamed again. Suddenly, the door to the phone booth opened and the weird cow appeared. Our eyes locked for a second, and I felt a glimmer of recognition, but before I could figure out who the cow was, it had grabbed the sack off the floor and disappeared out the side door.

I looked down at the pile of arms and legs and paws. I saw some blood begin to cover a yellow puppy ear, and I thought for sure I would faint. But I did not. I muttered some words that flew into my mind, and instead of sinking to the floor, I was heading toward the ceiling. First, I could feel my braids float up, and then my body followed. "Hey, guys," I yelled, "look at me!"

The pile of fists and thumping legs splayed all over the floor suddenly came to rest. Simon was the first to get to his feet. For a second, he looked madly around the floor for his sack of treats, but then his eyes turned toward me. "What the hell!" he yelled, sounding as uncool as I had ever heard him.

Brian was the next to reach a standing position. Instinctively, he reached out and grasped my hand, but when my patent leather black shoes passed his knees, he let go. That was too bad. I was certain that if he'd held on, I could have brought him up with me. By the time Paul was upright, my head was grazing the ceiling and had set off some sort of loud emergency alarm, and the door to the gymnasium had opened. Now a throng of cats and dogs and magicians and witches and elves and Mickey and Minnie Mouses were staring at me. And so was Tinkerbell, who, even from my position, I could still see was sorely pissed.

When I hit the floor, I thought for sure I had broken every bone in my body. For crying out loud, what kind of witch was Sarah? She obviously was good enough to have gotten me up in the air with no problems, but her ability to provide her students with a safe descent was sorely lacking. My right leg hurt like crazy.

There was an enormous flutter of activity as a horde of animals and comic creatures raced to my side. The first one to reach me was, of course, Brian, who had already figured out some way to turn off the alarm my head had triggered. With a most impressive touch of authority, he ordered, ''Move back and give the kid a chance to breathe.'' I was so touched by the gentle manner in which he lifted me and looked into my eyes that I wanted to kiss him on the spot. But there was no time for that. There were too many teachers and parents checking me over and kids staring and chattering for us to have a chance for even the smallest of kisses. Despite the questions and concerns of the adults, I could hear the voices around me.

"What did she just do?" "Did you see her fly?" "What kind of costume is that Dorothy outfit anyhow?" "Is that really Emily Silver?" I wanted to tell them all that I had just levitated and it was no big deal if they just practiced the instructions my mother had received from her friend, a local witch named Sarah Goody, but I decided to keep my mouth closed. I smiled as much as I could, despite the pain in my right leg.

When the teachers decided I was not completely crippled and could stand on my own, I was allowed to walk back into the gymnasium, supported around my waist by Brian and followed by an entourage of animals and weirdly dressed humans. As I was propelled forward, I turned around and saw the bum and Tinkerbell talking. The bum looked especially pale and Tinkerbell looked especially mad. I wanted to walk over to them, but I had little choice but to move forward.

A few minutes after my group finally got settled in the gym, Miss Marshall, the vice principal of the school, led me and Brian aside. My leg still ached, but as long as Brian was beside me, I could walk just fine. "Could you please explain to me what just happened?" she asked me in her singsong voice, which I had always thought was a bit unusual for a teacher whose main purpose in life was to assign students to detention hall. "There seems to be some confusion about exactly what you were just doing."

"I was practicing my jumps for cheerleading," I told her. "You see, a friend of my mother's who is a professional cheerleading coach told me that if I did a special type of breathing exercise and worked very hard on increasing my ankle strength, then I could jump as high as the ceiling. I'm happy with soccer, but I've been thinking maybe I might try out for cheerleading next year. Anyhow, I told Brian about it, and of course he thought I was nuts, so I had to prove it to him, and that's what I was doing out there. I almost fainted when I jumped so high I actually hit the ceiling. My ankle strength is unbelievable. I can hardly wait to tell my mother's friend about it. I mean, can you believe it?''

"Not easily," Miss Marshall said. Now she was looking at Brian's right floppy ear. "Is that blood on your ear?" she asked him.

"It could be," he answered. "I got a bloody nose when Emily started to jump so high. I get bloody noses whenever I'm in a plane. It's a real problem."

Miss Marshall was now directing all her energy toward Brian. I'd seen her in action several times, and I knew she could be downright mean. But at that moment, she didn't look scary, just confused and tired. "Are you all right, Brian?" she asked him, and he nodded firmly. "And you, Emily. Are you all right?" I nodded just as firmly. "Then I guess there's nothing to worry about. Some students were just a bit startled to see you jumping so high. I'd prefer it if you practiced your cheerleading jumps outside from now on, if you don't mind."

"No problem," I assured her.

"Then, let's go have a good time," she said, and a big smile formed on her face. I was as amazed as when I'd touched the ceiling.

Brian and I had just started to dance together when the lights were turned down low and our class adviser, Mrs. Driscoll, got up to hand out the awards. Carrie suddenly appeared at my side. She no longer looked mad. Just terribly unhappy. And alone. "Are you okay?" I asked, so grateful to see her near me that I had to restrain myself from kissing her.

"No," she said softly.

"Where's Simon?" I asked her, and she shook her head and shrugged her shoulders.

"I can't find him anywhere," she said. "Paul says he doesn't know where he went. I guess he just took off."

I had my arm around Carrie's shoulders, and Brian had his hand, or paw, tightly wrapped around my waist when Mrs. Driscoll called out our two names as the winning costume couple. I wasn't surprised. Everything wonderful and horrendous was happening to me that night. Why not this? I removed my arm from Carrie's tutu, and Brian and I walked quickly, hand in hand, up to the stage and received our awards, two huge chocolate kisses. And then the lights came back on and the band started playing again, and Brian and I danced, and Carrie stood there all alone. I was so happy in Brian's arms I could barely stand it, but it broke my heart to look at Carrie's face.

The music lasted for only one more song and the dance was suddenly and completely over. As Brian and Carrie and I walked out of the gym, we noticed a big pile of discarded flasks. "I might be starting to have hallucinations," we heard one guy mutter to his friend as he threw his flask onto the pile. "I mean, I think I saw that cute girl with the pigtails fly. I better hold up on the drinking for a while."

"You did it, Carrie," I said. "You got them to stop drinking for one night. And maybe even for longer than that."

Carrie smiled. A sad but sweet smile. "You're the

perfect queen,'' she whispered into my ear. "And your king adores you.'' I wasn't sure about a lot that had happened that night, but I was positive that my best friend's words were the truth.

eleven
𝒟

After Brian and I dropped Carrie off, we went for a little ride. I was certain that he was going to take me to Flax Pond, where Rockmere kids always made out. The thought of making out with Brian was so exciting and so scary that I could barely concentrate on our conversation.

"I don't think I understand anything about what happened tonight," Brian was saying while I was freaking out, trying to remember if Carrie had told me to kiss with my lips open or closed. I knew Carrie might feel bad if I called to ask her, but I was desperate. I hoped she'd be as understanding as she had been when Brian and I were named the winning costume couple. I was feeling very lucky to have such a good friend as Carrie and also wondering whether I could ask Brian to stop at Friendly's so I could call her about my lips, when he pulled his car into the Friendly's parking lot. "Are you as hungry as I am?" he asked as he turned off the engine. "I'm starved."

I was disappointed but grateful, sad but thrilled. I was dying to make out with him, but I had no idea how to manage such a feat. With luck, I could get to a phone and ask Carrie a few key questions while he munched on his bacon burger and french fries. "Sure," I answered. "I'm a little hungry."

For the next hour, I never left my seat. Instead, I sat beside Brian in the Friendly's booth while we talked and talked and talked. I never imagined that it could be so easy, but talking to Brian wasn't all that different from talking to Carrie. He was funny and smart and listened to what I said. Plus, he was incredibly interested in Simon.

"We were good friends up until last year," Brian told me. "Then he went his way and I went mine."

"I never knew that," I said, amazed at the thought of the two of them together. I'd never seen them together at school. "But for the past two or three years, Simon has never brought any friends home."

"He came over to my house quite a few times," Brian said. "We went to a lot of movies together and played ball. He was a terrific soccer player. He just didn't want to go to practices. But that was Simon. I hated to see the way he changed, his cheating on tests and drinking and being obnoxious to most of the guys he used to hang out with. There's something going on with him. I feel really bad about what happened tonight."

"He probably didn't even know it was you in the doggy costume," I said. We were still in our costumes, and I was glad he had washed the blood from his ear. He had taken off the head of the dog costume, and his own head looked just perfect to me. "I'm sure he would have felt terrible if he knew that."

"Oh, no, he wouldn't," Brian said. "I don't think there's a lot that makes Simon feel bad these days. I have to tell you, Emily. I'm worried about him. I'm sure you are, too."

"I've been worried about my brother since the day

I was born," I said. "But the past few years have been rough on all of us."

"He sure has gotten much worse this past year," he said. "And Paul's not the greatest friend for him right now. I just wish I were still his friend and could help him."

"I wish you were still his friend, too," I said. "I can't think of a better friend to help him come to his senses and get rid of Paul."

"I hate to worry you, Emily," he said, "but I just get a scary feeling inside when I think about Simon. He was awful tonight. He really frightened me."

"Don't give up on him," I said. "Promise me you won't." I don't know why I felt so intensely about Brian and Simon, but at that moment I was desperate.

Brian put down the chocolate Fribble he had been drinking and put his arm around me. It felt strong and warm and perfectly terrific. I still had no idea what to do with my lips if he kissed me, but I had a wonderful feeling that whatever I did with them would be okay. "Don't you worry, Emily," he said, drawing me closer to him. "I'm here for you." And then he kissed me. And I tasted chocolate Fribble and my lips stayed shut and the kiss felt delicious. Even more delicious than the Fribble, which was my ultimate favorite drink in the whole world.

When Brian brought me home an hour later, I had had two more tastes of Brian's Fribble, and I was convinced I was a natural born kisser. Brian offered me yet one more kiss before he left my front doorstep, promising to call me the next morning before he left for my dad's hardware store.

My mother was waiting for me in the kitchen, still wearing her black outfit, sipping a cup of flowery-smelling tea. She smiled when she saw me, but I could see the worry in her eyes. "Well, how was your evening?" she asked me. "I thought Brian was even cuter than the last time I saw him."

"Even in his doggy costume?" I asked her.

"Absolutely," she said. "You two looked adorable together."

"He'd love to be friends with Simon again," I told her. "But after what happened tonight, I don't think that's going to happen that easily. Simon brought a lot of alcohol to the dance, and Brian was responsible for Simon's not getting to spread it around."

"Oh, no." My mother gasped. "Did Simon get into trouble?"

"Not really," I assured her. "He just sort of disappeared before the situation got out of hand."

She looked at the kitchen clock. It was a few minutes before midnight. We both knew that midnight was Simon's curfew and that he rarely respected it. "Daddy went to sleep," she told me. "But I'm not tired. I think I'll wait up till Simon gets home."

"You look tired," I said.

"And you look adorable," she said, trying to change the subject. "Tell me more about your night."

I wanted to tell her about my levitation and the Fribble kiss and how wonderful Brian made me feel, but I knew her worry over Simon had taken over her mind. It could all wait till tomorrow—when, I hoped, she wouldn't be as worried. "It was perfect," I said. "But I'm too tired to stay up one second longer. I'll tell you everything in the morning." Her kiss tasted fruity. I wondered if I would ever get a kiss that was plain and tasteless.

I fell right asleep, but all night long I had weird dreams. Mostly about Simon, who seemed to be locked in a red room and needed me to find some stupid key. He was still wearing his Grateful Dead T-shirt and the rest of his bum costume, which I was beginning to suspect was no costume. In the morning, I was as exhausted as I had been when I went to sleep.

When I found my mother lying on the couch in our family room, dressed in the same black outfit she'd been wearing when I went to sleep, I knew Simon had not come home. I stared at my mother for a few minutes before she opened her eyes and saw me. She sat right up. "Simon didn't come home last night," she told me, and I nodded. "I called Sarah a half hour ago and she said for us to come over at noon. Will you come with me?"

"Sure, if you want," I said.

"Of course, he could come home before then," she said, rubbing her eyes. Man, did she look exhausted. "Knowing your brother, he'll just show up any minute and try to convince me he was sleeping in his bed all night."

I could see how hard she was trying, and I couldn't stand it. I could see the truth in her eyes. She was worn out with worry and lack of sleep. I was just so sick of the game we were playing. "He's in trouble, Mom," I told her. "I'm sure he's in some sort of real trouble this time."

"Oh, my God." She gasped. "You really think so?"

"Yes, I do," I said. "What did Daddy say?"

"He just shook his head and said he was sure Simon would come home when he slept off the booze, and then he went to the store. But you're right. I know you are. Something's terribly wrong, just like Sarah said."

When the phone rang, we both jumped as if a bomb had gone off. My mother beat me to the phone. "It's for you," she whispered as she handed it to me. "It's that precious Brian."

"Your dad told me Simon didn't come home last night," Brian said. "I guess he took off right off after your flight. What can I do to help find him?"

"Nothing," I told him. "I really appreciate your offer, but at noon my mother and I are going over to visit a friend of hers who can help us." I felt ridiculous telling him we were going to a witch's house. "She does a lot with missing people, and she'll help us for sure."

"I'd like to go with you," Brian said. "If that's okay with your mom and her friend, that is."

"That's so sweet of you to offer, Brian," I told him, "but my mom and I will be fine with just the two of us. Honestly, it probably makes more sense . . ." I was having trouble concentrating on what I was saying because my mother was moving up and down, waving her hands in front of my face and mouthing words I could not understand. "Excuse me a second," I said to Brian, covering the mouthpiece of the phone. "What's the matter?" I whispered to my mother, who looked ready to rip the phone out of my hand.

"Tell him to come," she said. "I want Brian to come with us. He used to be a good friend of Simon's, and he's a terrific young man, and we need all the help we can get. Please ask him to come."

This was insane. I knew it was insane. Plus, I felt weird about seeing Jeremiah and Brian together again. They hadn't exactly enjoyed each other's company at the lawn mower sale. It was just easier for me to keep the two of them separate. But I felt helpless to argue. "You know, that would probably be a great idea," I told Brian once my mother gave me some breathing space. "You should definitely come with us. If you still want to, I mean."

"I'll pick you up at a quarter to twelve," he told me. "If that gives us enough time to get to your mom's friend's house. I got here early this morning, so your father said I could take plenty of time off for lunch."

"That'll be fine," I said, happy for the chance to see Brian despite the craziness surrounding my life. Somehow, I'd manage being with the two guys again. "We'll be ready."

And we were. It wasn't until Brian pulled his car into Derby Street that I told him Sarah Goody was a witch. My mother was sitting in the front seat beside Brian, and I was in the back seat. The two of them had chatted about Simon the whole trip into Salem. Brian had talked about the time he and Simon borrowed George Freedman's moped and gone to Rockport. They hadn't been wearing helmets and had gotten pulled over. They'd had to call Brian's father to come get them and buy them helmets before the police would let them go back home. It sounded like they'd had a lot of fun, even in the police station waiting for Brian's dad.

Brian also talked about Simon's love of the Three Stooges and the way the two of them used to pretend they were Moe and Curly. I couldn't believe I'd never known about Brian and the moped and the Three Stooges. But my mother hadn't, either. It was amazing how little we knew about Simon's having fun. Mostly all we knew about was Simon's having trouble.

Brian took the idea of a visit to a witch's house pretty well. "Oh, sure," he said casually as we walked up the stairs to Sarah's front door. "I've heard of Sarah Goody. She's pretty well known, I think."

When Jeremiah opened the door, however, Brian seemed to lose a bit of his good humor. Actually, Jeremiah didn't look any happier to see Brian than Brian did to find Jeremiah opening the door. As for me, I didn't know which guy to look at, so I looked at my sneakers—which, I noticed, were untied. A few seconds later, however, I saw that they were tied. I was Dorothy back in the land of Oz, only this time without my pigtails.

"My mother is waiting for you in the living room," Jeremiah greeted us, speaking rather formally. "Actually, she would like to speak to Emily alone for a few minutes. If the two of you wouldn't mind waiting in the kitchen, I'd be glad to make you a cup of tea."

"Oh, I'd love some tea, too," I said as Jeremiah ushered us into the front hall. The last thing I wanted was to be alone with Sarah. I felt my finger. The wart had definitely shrunk away to nothing. But that didn't assure me at all. "I'm just so thirsty. I don't know if I've ever been this thirsty before."

There was something about this house that made me incredibly nervous, and something about Jeremiah that made me incredibly mouthy. The guy looked gorgeous in his back jeans and short-sleeved black T-shirt. Brian was adorable, and I was dying to kiss him again the minute I squished myself into the back seat of his car. But Jeremiah was darkly handsome and very sexy.

I couldn't understand how I could be attracted to both these guys. But I was. And the strangest part of it all was that they both appeared to be attracted to me. This was far stranger than shoelaces tying or lockers opening by themselves. Suddenly, I thought of Carrie and I wondered if it was fair that I was wrapped up in both these guys. Maybe I should give her one. Or maybe Simon, by some miracle, could make her happy. It was weird, but looking at Jeremiah in the soft light of the hallway, he looked a little like Simon, especially around the eyes and the mouth. Jeremiah was probably two years older than my brother. I'd never noticed it before, but the resemblance was quite apparent.

"No problem," Jeremiah assured me. "I'll bring you a cup of tea once you get settled in the living room." He was acting so formal and sure of himself that he seemed even older than he looked. I waited for my mother to say I didn't have to be alone with Sarah in the dark, scary living room while she and Brian had a tea party in the bright cheerful kitchen. But she said nothing. She just smiled calmly at Jeremiah.

Brian didn't look any more comfortable than I felt. "How about I go into the living room with your mother and Emily," he suggested. "Simon and I used to be good friends, and I might be able to help her find him."

"Perhaps later," Jeremiah said firmly as he opened the door to the kitchen for my two escorts. "But now it will be just Emily." For a minute I was certain Brian was going to say something else, but when my mother put her hand on his sleeve, he said nothing. Great. Let the two of them drink their happy tea while I got shipped off to the dark side of the moon. Still, when Jeremiah put his hand on my waist and directed me toward the living room, I didn't feel all that unhappy. I saw the look Brian was giving me: miserable—and, quite possibly, jealous. I took a deep breath, sucked in my stomach as much as I could, and followed my gladiator into the ring.

Sarah was sitting in the big armchair. Her eyes were

barely open, and she looked more asleep than awake. But her voice was remarkably strong. "I'm so glad you could come, Emily," she greeted me. "Please sit down. We need to get right to work. Your brother, as you well know, got himself into a difficult position last night. We were able to remove him from that situation, but now it appears as if he has slipped away from us."

"Us?" I hated to interrupt, but I felt it was important to stay with this woman as long as I could. If she took off for another out-of-body experience, I couldn't follow. If she levitated, I might be able to stay with her. But I had to know what she was talking about. "Who is 'us'?"

"Jeremiah and me," she answered. I glanced at Jeremiah, who smiled cutely. He didn't look as formal or old when he smiled. He just looked gorgeous. "Jeremiah was at the dance, dressed as a cow. He managed to remove your brother from the problem by helping you levitate and by getting rid of the alcohol. When he was trying to bring Simon to our house, Simon escaped from Jeremiah's car. Jeremiah has been trying to find him all night and all morning, but he's had no luck."

I took another glance at Jeremiah. For someone who had been up all night, he sure looked well rested. And the cow bit didn't surprise me at all. I'd thought that cow looked familiar. I was a bit diappointed to find out that I hadn't managed the levitation by myself, but I was certain that with a little more practice I'd be up there in no time. I was proud of myself. It was taking a lot to throw me now. Or maybe I was just so far gone nothing could push me any further over the edge. "I really appreciate all your help," I said, smiling at Jeremiah, who smiled back. Man, was

I glad I wasn't in the kitchen. Man, was I crazy. "But maybe we should just call the police and see if they can find him."

"Of course, we could do that," Sarah said. "But right now, I feel I have a better chance of finding him than they do."

And then it hit me. "I saw him," I told them. "I saw Simon in a dream last night. He was in a red room but he couldn't find the key, and he wanted me to help him."

"I knew he would try and reach you," Sarah said. I glanced back at Jeremiah, expecting to see another beautiful smile on his face, but this time there was no smile. If anything, he looked sad. Or mad. The guy was unbelievable. He was that upset over my brother's situation. Brian was great, but this guy was out of this world.

"I knew from the very beginning that I couldn't help Simon escape the danger completely," Sarah continued, while I smiled at Jeremiah to let him know how grateful I was for his caring about my brother so much. "I knew he would have to face it and be saved. That's why I drew the shield around you. And gave you special powers, so you could help him. Now that your dream shows you have a connection to him, that's what you have to do."

"Are you sending me into the red room?" I asked. I was scared, but having Jeremiah beside me helped. "I'll do whatever you want me to do."

"You are such a brave, dear girl," Sarah said. "But don't worry. I'm not going to put you in danger. I just need you to help me find Simon so I can make certain he doesn't get into any more danger. Even though Jeremiah was able to take away that sack your brother had filled with alcohol, Simon might have stored more alcohol somewhere else and could be drinking heavily now. I want you to close your eyes and let me try to bring you to where he is. It will be good for him to see you."

I closed my eyes and shook my head. I had no idea what this woman was going to do to me. Perhaps she was putting me on a plane and sending me to the land of the red room. Or maybe I was going to have an out-of-body experience and arrive there without my body. Or maybe she was collapsing me into a bottle and casting me out upon the sea, where I would ride the waves until I got to the red room. It didn't matter. I was someone special, someone whom the handsome Jeremiah and the adorable Brian found worth smiling at.

Sleepiness overcame me like a shot from an anes-thesiologist, and I let my body fall into a graceful heap upon the love seat, my head snuggled dreamily against Jeremiah's shoulder, my heart beating against his, my right hand locked between his two beautiful hands. I was in orbit and it didn't matter if I ever came back to earth.

twelve

When *I opened my eyes, I was still seated on the love* seat next to Jeremiah. It took me a minute to get my bearings. For what had seemed like a very long time, I had floated around somewhere, escaping the attacks of fierce-looking enemies with pointed heads, scissor-like nails, and Dracula teeth. Nothing seemed definite, but I knew I had been chased and assaulted and in constant danger. Somehow, I had managed to elude my hideous opponents, and now I was feeling even stronger and more perfect than before. At the same time, I had no memory of Simon or the red room. I had no idea where I had been or what I had seen or done, but I was very glad to be back exactly where I was.

Sarah and Jeremiah were staring at me hesitantly, almost as if there was something they wanted to say to me. "Well, I'm back," I told them, wondering if it would be okay if I returned to the kitchen and my mother and Brian. Not that I wasn't happy to be around Jeremiah, but I did sort of miss them. But I could tell these two weren't through with me, so I leaned back in the chair and closed my eyes. I was getting the hang of how these people operated. They'd talk when they were ready. Or send me off somewhere or bring me back when they were ready. It seemed useless to fight them. Plus, I was awfully tired from wherever it was they'd sent me.

Jeremiah began, as I knew he would. "My mother would like a chance to try and explain some of what has been happening to you. We had hoped to talk to you and your mother, but when you brought your little friend with you, it was a bit more difficult for us to talk privately. If it's all right with you, I'm going to ask Brian to leave and have your mother join us here for a talk."

"But Brian's a very good friend of mine, and he was kind enough to drive us here," I said, not thrilled with the idea of Brian's taking off and leaving Mom and me in Salem. Plus, it wasn't nice of Jeremiah to talk so meanly of Brian, who was just so adorable. But Jeremiah did look darned hunky. There was no doubt I was out of my mind. "I mean, how will we get home when we're through?"

Jeremiah smiled. "I'll take you home, of course," he said.

And I couldn't seem to get my eyes off that smile, no matter how hard I tried. I nodded and finally closed my eyes, feeling as if I were being carried off to somewhere far, far away. The next thing I knew my mother was sitting next to me and I felt as if I had just woken up from a nice, relaxing nap. Man, was I being rude with all these little naps. I'd had no idea I was so tired. "Well, hi, sweetie," my mom said, looking a little worried and brushing my bangs off my forehead. I usually hated it when she did that, but at that moment it felt good. I had the strangest feeling that I'd just heard something very unsettling, even though I couldn't remember exactly what it was. But

I did pick up a delicious aroma that smelled vaguely familiar and incredibly wonderful. I breathed in deeply and felt even more invigorated. "You've been asleep for quite a while, you know," Mom added.

I glanced at my watch. She wasn't exaggerating. I'd been out for over an hour. I sat up straighter in my seat. Jeremiah and Sarah were there, in the same seats they'd been in before, but they both looked tired, as my mom did, as if they needed the nap I'd just had. "What did I miss?" I asked, glancing from one face to the next. "I know it was important."

"It was," my mother agreed. "I wanted to wake you, but you just looked so tired, I couldn't bear to. I guess you didn't get much sleep either last night. I'll collapse later, I can assure you. But Jeremiah and Sarah have something important to tell us." She glanced at the two of them. "Anytime you two are ready, Emily and I would love to hear what you have to say." My mother sounded different. Not just tired but unemotional, which was not her usual state.

Sarah turned to Jeremiah, patted him on the knee gently, and then began to speak to Mom and me. Her voice was strong and full of an energy I did not share, but I found myself fascinated with every word she spoke. "This is not easy for me or for Jeremiah. I am Simon's birth mother. I had no idea that Ellen was my biological son's adoptive mother when she called me to arrange the interview. I only came to realize this when I did her past life regression and picked up a few hints that the two of us were strongly connected in our present lives. But the truth is, there are no accidents in life. Everything happens for a reason."

I looked at my mother. She was speechless. I was flabbergasted by Sarah's words, but I was much more concerned with my mother's reaction. "Are you okay, Mom?" I asked nervously.

She nodded and reached out to hold my hand. "Please continue, Sarah," she said in a voice far smaller than Sarah's.

Sarah glanced at Jeremiah before continuing. He did not look happy, but he, too, nodded. I wondered if this was the first time he was hearing this story. "Jeremiah knows this story very well," Sarah said, and I wasn't the least bit surprised that she had taken a quick trip into my brain. "I had been living in Seattle when Simon was born. I was about to divorce my husband and did not feel capable of raising this baby. You see, I already had another child with my husband, a son two years older than Simon, whom I left with my husband after Simon was born and the divorce was final. That son is Jeremiah Brooks."

Sarah stopped talking. My mother stared at Jeremiah. He offered her a slight smile, but it wasn't one of those nice smiles he usually showed. It was, actually, a sad, sort of nasty smile. Jeremiah was Simon's brother. Sarah was Simon's mother. I was Simon's sister. It wasn't easy, but I was struggling to stay with the program.

"I must sound like a terrible woman to you," Sarah was saying. "And I suppose I was. It was very difficult for my husband to allow our second son to be adopted. But he knew he would have an impossible time caring for a two-year-old and an infant by himself. I was just beginning to feel my powers, and it scared my husband that I could do strange things like levitate and know what he was going to say before he said it. The poor man was frightened of me. He adored Jeremiah and probably was afraid I was going to take him away from him, too. I tried hard to make him understand that I would be a terrible mother to sons. I know this is hard for you to understand, but I sensed that if my children had been female, I would have been able to have stayed with them. I thought then, that as a wicca, or witch, I could raise only daughters, not sons. I believed that only females possessed the magical abilities I possessed.'' Jeremiah looked away from her glance. ''I was wrong,'' she continued, her voice a bit softer. ''But at that time, for my sons' sakes, I felt I needed to let them go. I wanted them to have normal childhoods, and I believed I was not the person to make that happen.'' She stopped, looking as if she'd finally run out of words.

But Jeremiah had plenty more. ''I was two when she left,'' he said, sounding sad. I could hear some anger mixed in with the sadness. ''When she was seven months pregnant, she left Seattle and moved to Boston, where she hired a lawyer to handle the adoption. He knew your family and told her about you. She liked everything she heard and decided you would be the best possible parents Simon could have. The lawyer arranged everything so you could take Simon home from the hospital when he was three days old.

''After she left the hospital, Sarah came to Salem. The minute she arrived, she knew this was where she belonged. She formed her own coven and devoted her energies to becoming a powerful and effective witch, using her talents to help others in every way she could.'' Sarah's eyes were closed, and she looked sad. My mother's eyes were open, and she looked dazed.

But Jeremiah continued. ''My father told me she had died, and I accepted that. A year and a half ago, when I turned eighteen and was ready to go to college, he told me the truth. I wasn't surprised to hear that my mother was a witch. I'd always known I was different, that I could do things, like open locked doors and guess what people were thinking and what was inside packages. I felt different from my friends. But I was surprised to hear that she was living. Before I took off for Duke, I was determined to find her, and I did quite easily, with my father's help. And I've been living with her since."

"You were accepted at Duke University?" my mother asked with that reverential tone she always used when talking about the top colleges, and I felt a small wave of relief. The woman sitting next to me had not been demented by this astounding story about her son's origins. She was still my mother.

"Jeremiah deferred his acceptance so he could spend time getting to know me, but he plans to go to medical school after Duke," Sarah answered in nearly the same tone my mother had assumed when uttering "Duke." "One of Jeremiah's natural talents is his ability to work with the human body. He can perform many of the same medical feats I can. He will make an excellent physician. I am curious whether Simon also possesses some of these talents."

"Simon hates going to the doctor," my mother said. "The sight of blood terrifies him. I have a strong feeling he'll want to go into law."

"You could be right," Sarah said thoughtfully. "But I still see him doing something with medicine. Perhaps he'll specialize in medical law."

"He might even want to go into the hardware store business with his father," my mother said. "He loves working at the store." I nearly fell off my chair with that one. I didn't have to be a psychic witch to understand that my mother was exhibiting some unpleasant feelings toward Sarah Goody. Jeremiah, I could see at a glance, also was uncomfortable with the turn of the conversation.

"I'm certain Simon will be successful at whatever he chooses," Sarah continued, smiling warmly at both my mother and Jeremiah, neither one of whom smiled warmly back at her. "That is what all of us want for him. But we can all understand how difficult his life has been. Not just as the only adopted sibling in a family, but as a young man with magical powers he doesn't comprehend. I'd always suspected that my second-born son had both powers and problems, but it wasn't until I met Ellen last week that it all became clear to me. The more involved I became with the two of you, the more I was able to see the oncoming problems with him. I could see—"

"Where is he?" my mother interrupted Sarah. Her patience had been stretched too far. "I'm trying to understand Simon's past, and believe me, it's not easy. But right now I'm much more concerned about his present." Her voice got soft and she was on the verge of tears. "You've lost him, haven't you?"

"Just temporarily," Sarah said. "Somehow he eluded Jeremiah after the dance ended. Strangely enough, you're the one he's come to, Emily, and you can help us find him. You want to do that, don't you?"

I wanted to go back to sleep. I wanted to go back to Friendly's with Brian. I wanted to dance with Jeremiah at the Halloween dance. I wanted to smell more of the tantalizing aroma surrounding me. I didn't know what I wanted. But I was certain I didn't want to go into some stupid red room and sit there with my brother. "Sure," I lied. I'd have said anything to get out of that house.

"Good," Sarah said, smiling warmly at me. "Because during your nap, I was able to increase your psychic talents so that you can find him and bring him home. You look well rested now and should be able to concentrate on finding your brother. Do you feel up to that now, dear?"

What I felt up to was getting into Jeremiah's car and going home—and maybe concentrating on getting the police to concentrate on getting my brother home. Of course, I wanted my mother to feel better, but a return trip to the red room was not on my itinerary that day. "Sure," I lied again. "But are you sure the police can't help us, too? I mean, I'm perfectly willing to do this alone, but I have no problem taking a policeman along with me, if that's okay with all of you."

"Unfortunately, the police can't help," Jeremiah said, and I got a funny feeling as he spoke. He just didn't seem all that anxious to help find my—or, rather, our—brother. "Simon's had enough little tangles with them that they see him as a wild kid who likes to drink and get into trouble. You live in a small town, Emily, and I'm sure they heard about the scene at the dance. The last thing we want is for them to decide Simon was responsible for the alcohol that was brought into the dance. Who knows? Maybe Simon isn't in any great danger. Maybe he doesn't want to come home and is pretending to be locked up. I'm just not certain."

I looked at Jeremiah and got the same funny feeling again. I wasn't sure if it was this new psychic power Sarah had given me, but I sensed that Jeremiah Brooks wasn't as concerned about bringing my brother back as the rest of us were.

My mother, however, had no such psychic power.

"I bet Jeremiah is right and he's pretending to be locked up," she said, perking right up. "I'm even going to tell your father Simon called and is at Paul's ski house in New Hampshire for the weekend. That will give us today and tomorrow for you to find the miserable kid and get him home."

"Sure," I agreed, closing my suddenly heavy eyes for just a second. When I opened them, the delicious scent that had been teasing me to distraction was gone. And so was Jeremiah. But Sarah, who was now sitting beside me, had her own unique smell. I swear, it had that frankincense stuff in it, too. But she also smelled like olive oil and salt. I took a deep breath. Actually, she smelled like a steak marinade my dad liked. Maybe Sarah was a famous chef, as well as a witch. All I knew for sure was that I felt just fine. Just dandy. And ready to go wherever this weird-smelling woman wanted me to.

"Why don't you just relax for a second longer, Emily," Sarah suggested. "I know this is a very tense time for you and your mother. I have told you things that have disturbed you greatly, but I need you both to be calm and focused on finding Simon. I was in the middle of showing your mother a pendulum exercise when you woke up. It helped her relax and focus, and I think it could help you, too."

"Sure," I answered as she took a small round crystal out of her pocket. The crystal dangled from a string which Sarah held a couple of feet above my mother's head. Beautiful rays of light shone off the crystal and danced off Sarah's dark walls. I couldn't take my eyes off it.

"You just relax now, Ellen," Sarah told my mother, who was looking awfully relaxed already, slumped in one of Sarah's living room chairs.

Her eyes were open, but she sure looked sleepy. "Breathe deeply from your diaphragm and belly." Slowly, Sarah began to swing the crystal over my mother's head. Then, a minute or so later, she lowered it so it was practically touching my mother's black curls. I watched, mesmerized, as the crystal swung in a circular motion. "That's wonderful, Ellen," Sarah said. "But now, let's switch. You be the receiver, and I'll be the sender."

My mother nodded and stood, slowly vacating her chair for Sarah, who sat down, closed her eyes, and breathed deeply for a few minutes. "Ready," she said, and my mother began to swing the crystal above Sarah's head of long, wild, black hair. Again, the crystal started to move in a circular motion, seemingly motivated by a spirit of its own, unaffected by the motions of my mother's wrist. "Now I am the sender, and you are the receiver," Sarah said, and my mother nodded and closed her eyes. "I am giving you the energy and strength you need and taking away your tension. You are in a room of glass, a city of glass. Towers of glass rise up from under the sea and colored fish swim through the clear glass walls. Everywhere around you there is light and beauty."

There was silence in the room for a good ten minutes while the crystal swung around and around, and my mother stood smiling, and Sarah sat without emotion, and I sat staring, wondering if I could just grab the crystal and hold it above my own head for a few minutes. But nobody suggested I be part of the ceremony, so I held my hands tightly at my sides and thought about Brian and Jeremiah and Carrie and soccer and Simon and my father's lawn mower sale.

Suddenly, Sarah and the crystal were in front of my face, and I was breathing deeply and my mind cleared, and all I could think about was a bright sunny sky that was so blue it took my breath away. And the pretty colored fish danced in the sea of azure glass.

"Tell us about the dance last night, Emily," Sarah suggested as she slipped the crystal back into her pocket, and I nodded.

So we sat there, the three of us, on a lovely, fall Saturday afternoon, in Sarah's charming living room, chatting about the weather and me. "I had a great time," I said. "Brian is just so sweet. And everybody kept asking me to dance. I was the belle of the ball."

"And you looked so beautiful," Sarah told me. "You made a precious Dorothy."

"That she did," my mother agreed. I was surprised that Sarah knew how I'd looked.

"You were there?" I asked her.

"Oh, no." Sarah laughed lightly. "Jeremiah told me. He said you were the prettiest girl there. Even prettier than your friend Carrie."

"She did look adorable," my mother said. She still had the weird, kind of stunned look on her face she'd had ever since Sarah had told us about Simon, obviously still in the process of registering all we'd learned. The crystal pendulum exercise had calmed her down a bit. I had no idea why, but she was beginning to remind me of the colored fish I'd just met. If the two of us ever got out of this house with some of our two minds intact, I knew we would have long, serious discussions about Sarah and Simon and Jeremiah and the fish. "You know, it's amazing the way Simon reached you," my mom continued, in a voice I would not describe as her usual one. "I still can't get over his calling you. Obviously, he is closer to you than any of us realized."

"That's true," Sarah said, and we all nodded. I was

getting a little bit of a headache from all the nodding.

"I just don't know how to handle that boy," Sarah continued, while I smiled agreeably and nodded. "Keeping him out of trouble is almost an impossible job. First I gave Emily all those herbs to sprinkle on his bed and clothes and in his shower. Then I had Jeremiah give him an amulet made from bird feathers and alfalfa sprouts. But none of those made any difference with him. I made him a beautiful steel talisman out of Solomon's Seal with two superimposed triangles. It's used to protect cars and motor equipment, but I had a feeling it would be good for him. I even drew a tetragrammation on the floor of the gym in chalk, but Jeremiah said Simon erased it with his foot. Then I went to your house and attached a protection philter underneath his bed that I made out of patchouli oil, frankincense, wolf's hair, sandalwood powder, cinquefoil leaves, and some powdered myrrh. I also made a little extra, put it in a black muslin bag, and hung it on his door. Unfortunately, Simon sneezed and choked so badly that Jeremiah had to go back later and remove nearly all of it.

"After that, I had Jeremiah hammer iron nails that I'd charged into the frame of Simon's bedroom window. But Jeremiah said Simon removed them. That boy does have his powers. Possibly more than I possess. We were visualizing a sleeping dragon with its shiny green body curled around the room when you woke up, Emily. It would be nice if you could join us for a second. Just imagine the dragon awakening if anyone comes to harm Simon. Make his skin green and shiny. Give him super hot fire breath and a gigantic long tail. Can you do that, dear?"

Of course, I could do that. And that's exactly what I did for close to an hour. It was a lot easier than imagining Sarah or Jeremiah walking around my house attaching black muslin bags to doorknobs and nailing windows shut while I slept unaware in a nearby bedroom. I think I might actually have fallen asleep beside the sleeping dragon, because the next thing I knew it was dark in the room, and my mother was gone. There were some candles glowing on the table in front of me. I stood up slowly, feeling very unsteady on my feet, then sat back down and placed my head on the table. I had a wicked headache and a strong sense of confusion. I knew I was in Sarah's living room and that my mother and Sarah were gone, but that was all I could figure out. I must have fallen asleep again, because when I opened my eyes the candles were smaller.

"Emily. Come here, Emily." I heard the voice through the thick fog in my head. The scratchy feeling in my throat left little doubt who was calling me.

"Hi, Jeremiah," I answered sleepily. "Where are you?"

"Right here," he said. I opened my eyes as wide as I could, but I couldn't see him. All I could see were the stupid flickering candles. "Stand up and walk over to the doorway, and you'll see me."

I stood up and felt as dizzy as I had earlier, but I made my way, slowly and carefully, to the doorway between the kitchen and the dining room. I looked into the kitchen. There he was. The gorgeous Jeremiah. Dressed in black jeans and a black cotton cowboy-type shirt, leaning against a kitchen chair. "Come here," he said, and like an unsteady wind-up toy, I followed his directions. "That a girl. Come sit down, right here." First he sat down, and then I sat down, right on his lap. I closed my eyes and leaned against Jeremiah's strong body. I could feel the muscles through his shirt. This was one muscular dude. I was dizzy and confused. I was sitting in Jeremiah's lap. I wasn't sure that was where I wanted to be, but every time I tried to imagine where I did want to be, Jeremiah's presence overwhelmed me. Something was wrong with this picture, but I was darned if I could figure it out.

When Jeremiah wrapped his arms around me, half of me wanted to faint from happiness and the other half wanted to run away. "We have to talk," he said into my hair, and I nodded. "Are you able to listen to me?"

"Sure," I said. I forced myself to sit up straight. I had no intention of leaving Jeremiah's lap, yet I tried to push myself out. I wondered if I was developing a split personality. I wasn't sure if it was my imagination, but I thought I saw someone sitting in another chair at the opposite end of the kitchen, someone large and in black. "Are we alone? Just the two of us?"

"No," he answered. "Sarah's here. But she's having an out-of-body experience. She's in Boston. She'll be back soon. But I need you to listen to me. Okay?" I nodded. "You remember that Simon's missing, right?"

"Oh, I know that," I said, wondering what was going on. This guy looked and felt and smelled like Jeremiah, but how come he didn't know what Jeremiah knew? "He's been missing since Friday night at the dance. He got away from you. He was in the red room. Did you forget that?"

Jeremiah sat up straighter. I almost fell off his lap, but he held on to me. Then he picked me up, as easily as if I were a child, and placed me on a chair beside Sarah. Or beside the person who was Sarah but was in Boston. Part of me was hoping I'd be back in that lap in no time, and part of me wondered if it could get to Boston pronto. "He's no longer in the red room," Jeremiah told me, and all the soft, tingling lap feelings disappeared. It was Boston all the way. "I'm certain he disappeared a few hours ago. While you were having your little talk with Sarah and your mother, he managed to get out of the room. It's hard to believe, but he did it. And he's gone far, far away. My mother thinks he's in Boston, but I'm convinced he's much farther away than that."

"Where's my mother?" I asked. "Does she know this?"

"She's here. She's sleeping in one of the upstairs bedrooms. She doesn't know yet. But we'll have to tell her he could be beyond our reach now."

Up to that moment I'd felt as if I were still in some sort of a daze. Jeremiah's initial words had pierced through that daze, but the knowledge that my mother didn't know my brother had gotten even farther away from us increased whatever confusion I still felt. Would I ever be able to figure out what was going on? No part of me wanted to return to Jeremiah's lap now. I wanted to go back to my house. With my mother, father, and destructive brother. "What's happening with Simon?" I moaned pathetically. "Tell me, Jeremiah."

Jeremiah looked very sad. Amazingly, the sadness magnified his good looks. I wanted to kiss him. I wanted to go home. I wanted to go to Boston. I wanted to be normal, just for five minutes. "I don't know where to begin," he said.

"At the beginning," I suggested. "I'm still having trouble accepting the fact that my brother is Sarah's son. The son of a witch. Thousands of times I wished that his real parents would appear and take him away so my parents and I could live happily ever after, but I knew that was never going to happen. Why on earth would someone who'd given Simon away want him back? But Sarah is his mother! And he's your brother as well as mine. By the way, that doesn't mean you and I are related, does it?''

Jeremiah smiled sadly. ''It sure doesn't,'' he said. ''But I can understand how hard this is for you. I was amazed at how well you and your mother took it this afternoon.''

''We're still in shock,'' I assured him. ''But what about you and Simon? Don't you want to get to know your brother? It must be tough for you that he's missing since you just found out he was your real brother.''

Jeremiah kept giving me that same tender smile. I wanted to jump back on his lap and kiss him; I wanted to pummel him with my fists until he told me what was going on with Simon. ''Of course I want to get to know him,'' he said. ''Just the way Sarah does. All she's talked about since she met your mother is Simon. How things got so much worse with Simon a few years ago. How Simon had crossed the line from being difficult to becoming dangerous. How Simon's obsession with alcohol had grown much worse. I couldn't bear hearing it anymore. I finally promised to help her bring Simon back under control. You know, my life hasn't been that easy, either. But, unlike Simon, I've managed to keep my life on a normal keel. Of course I want to help our brother, Emily, but I also want to prepare you for the terrible fact that it might not be possible for you, or anyone, to help Simon. He may be beyond our reach now. And never coming back. Actually, I think Simon is no longer in any danger. He's just left us.''

Jeremiah seemed so sincere. And so angry. So gentle. And so nasty. Some of what he said didn't make sense. I couldn't put my finger on it but there was something terribly wrong. I knew I should be frightened for Simon, and I was. But I was getting awfully tired again. Every time I felt as if I was beginning to understand the confusion around me, my thoughts got blocked and I couldn't figure out anything. "Please tell me what you want me to do," I said, anxious to have him kiss me, anxious for him to take me home, anxious for my mind to start functioning normally again.

Suddenly, the woman sitting next to me in the kitchen cried out. A low, deep sigh. Jeremiah was at her side in a flash. "You're exhausted, Mother. Enough for today."

"I'm all right," she insisted, sitting perfectly upright in her chair, but she sure didn't look it. "I need to go back to Boston shortly. I'm very worried about him. Give me a minute to catch my breath, and I'm going back there."

"No, you're not," Jeremiah said firmly. "You've done enough for one day. I'll take over. Besides, I'm certain he's not in Boston. But if you insist, I'll go there and look for him. You go upstairs and rest. Please."

Sarah shook her head. "No, Jeremiah. I must go. You can't handle this. Only I can."

Jeremiah grabbed both of her hands in his and held them tightly. "No, Mother," he said firmly.

But she went to Boston. At least, I thought that's where she went. All I know for sure is that Sarah closed her eyes, muttered a few words, and then went limp. Either she'd gone back to Boston or she'd died, which I doubted since Jeremiah didn't offer CPR.

"Oh, God," he moaned instead. He sat there for a few minutes, head in his hands, looking totally miserable, while I sat in my chair wondering if I could possibly have an OBE myself and get out of that crazy house.

I stared at Sarah and wished she would take her body out of there and go experience someplace else. Quickly. And forever. I was getting darned sick of all this worry about Simon. Jeremiah seemed certain that Simon had gone away because he wanted to. Or had he? Had Simon gone so far away that none of us could bring him back? Was it time to forget Simon and go on with our lives? Was it time to stop listening to Jeremiah and call the police? Was it time to go swimming with the brightly colored little fishies again?

A voice behind me rescued me from my confusion. "Emily. Jeremiah. Sarah. What's going on here?" I turned around and saw my mother, looking like she had awakened from a deep sleep, standing in the dining room doorway. "Something terrible has happened to Simon. I know it for sure. Tell me what it is. Now."

thirteen
♌

$\mathcal{S}$*arah was still somewhere else, and it took a long time* for Jeremiah to get off the floor where he was kneeling beside his mother and lead my mother to a chair. "You're right, Ellen," he told her as she perched on the edge of the seat. Her curls were uncombed and wild, her face was pale and worried, and her black outfit was wrinkled and unkempt. So much for the great power of the pendulum and crystal. My mother looked awful. "Something *has* happened to Simon," Jeremiah continued, making the supreme effort to remove his eyes from his serene, probably sedated mother and concentrate on my frantic, distraught parent. "We're not at all sure where he is now. Perhaps in Boston. Perhaps New York or California. And Sarah is there now, trying to keep him safe."

"California!" my mother repeated. "What's he doing in California? And what is she doing about all this?" She glanced at Sarah, completely awake now.

"She's in Boston or New York or California," I told my mother. "You know, having an OBE."

"Oh, brother." My mother moaned. "Could someone just take us home so I can call the airlines and find my son?"

"Great idea . . ." I started to say, when Sarah came back from Boston.

"I'm getting nowhere," she said softly. "I don't understand it, but I'm just not getting near him. Something is keeping me away from him."

"It's because you're so tired," her adoring son told her. I wondered if it was possible that I could possibly be jealous of the concern and affection Jeremiah showed his mother. I was experiencing moments of extreme dislike for this guy, but I still felt urges to snuggle up next to that beefy bod. Man, was I one sick cookie. "Please go rest, Ellen, and I'll work with Emily and figure out how to get Simon back."

"I've had more than enough rest," my mother said firmly, standing up. "Emily's going home with me. I'm still reeling from everything you've told me. I appreciate everything you two have done, but I know a couple of places Simon likes to go to in Boston, and I'm sure Emily and I can find him there. He would never go to New York or California. Never."

"It's not that simple," Sarah said convincingly. "I hate to scare you, but there is an even greater danger facing Simon now. I cannot grasp exactly what it is, but someone or something wants to hurt Simon, and we must find him before he or it succeeds."

My mother sat down in a flash. Sarah's words had sent shivers down my spine, and my feelings about Simon were a lot less loving than my mother's. "Oh, God." She groaned. "What do we do now?" she asked so softly it was difficult to understand her words.

But Sarah had understood them. "We use Emily's power over her brother," she answered. "You're right, Ellen. You two should go home. I want you to sit in your room, Emily, until Simon reaches you. I'm certain he will find you there. He's aware something is wrong and he doesn't know who else to seek out. I've given you a great deal of ammunition to help you reach him. As soon as you hear from him, you must call me. And the police. Together, we'll bring him home safely. I'm certain he's trying to reach you now. Take them home, Jeremiah. And stay with Emily. She'll need you.''

My mother didn't say another word. She stood up, grabbed my hand, pulled me up from my chair, and followed Jeremiah out of the room. None of us spoke during the ride to our house. My mother sat beside Jeremiah in the front and I sat in the back. I was so exhausted all I wanted to do was take yet another nap. It was hard to believe that Sarah had given me any powers at all, except the power to fall asleep no matter where I was.

When we pulled into our driveway, my father's car was not there but Brian's was. My mother literally ran into the house. ''I'll be back in a few minutes,'' Jeremiah said as he helped me out of the BMW. ''I have a quick errand to run.'' He put both his hands firmly on my shoulders and stared into my eyes. ''No matter what happens, do not leave this house until I come back. No matter how long I am gone, you must stay here. Will you promise me that, Emily?'' I nodded. And ran into the house.

Brian was sitting on the couch in our family room. A plate of brownies, the real gooey chocolate-chip-and-marshmallow ones, was on the coffee table in front of him. Brian stood up. ''Your father let us in,'' he told my mother and me. ''He was worried that you guys weren't home yet, but he had to go back to the store. The lawn mowers are selling like crazy, and he's getting another shipment in tonight from a store in New Hampshire. He's having a big run on shovels, too. People are buying two or three at a time. He's never seen anything like it. I sent a couple of my friends to help him while I waited here. I hated to leave you in Salem, but that goon Jeremiah didn't give me much choice. If you didn't get home by nine, I was heading back there with the police.''

Suddenly, Carrie appeared in the doorway. I glanced back at the brownies. Of course. They were the ones she always makes. She rushed up to my mother and me and tried to wrap her arms around both of us. "Thank God, you're home!'' she cried as she hugged us. "I've been calling here all day. I finally found Brian at the hardware store and we decided to come here and wait for you two. He made me a nervous wreck with his descriptions of Sarah's house. Any luck with Simon? I'm *so* worried about him. Do you want a brownie? Please tell me what's going on.''

Carrie looked and sounded frantic. Her hair was a mess and she didn't even have any lipstick on. She reminded me of my mother. I tried to swallow my feelings about Carrie's and Brian's sitting there eating brownies, worrying about me and my mother and brother, just the two of them, all those hours. I hated having turned into such a jealous person. Maybe Sarah had sprinkled some jealousy powder into the mess she'd poured over me while I'd been napping.

"Simon's probably in Boston," my mother said simply. "Maybe New York or California. We're supposed to wait until he contacts Emily. And that's only part of what's going on with Simon. If you think I understand any of this, you're as crazy as the two of us.'' She looked so exhausted I was certain she would collapse if she didn't lie down.

"Mom,'' I said firmly, once I unwrapped Carrie's

arms from around my body, "please go lie down. Just for a half hour. In case Simon does try to reach me, the four of us will go find him. Or call the police, I promise. We'll wait for you. Just go rest for a little while."

I knew she didn't want to lie down, but she was so worn out she had no choice. "Just for a half hour," she told me. "Then we're going to call your father and sit down and decide what to do." I nodded, and she hugged Carrie and me and left the room. I was tempted to help her up the stairs, but she managed to climb them on her own. Never had I seen my mother so wiped out.

Suddenly, I felt an overpowering need to lie down and close my eyes. Without a word to Carrie or Brian, I lay on the couch, closed my eyes, and saw him. Simon. I couldn't believe it. He was still in the red room. "Hurry up, Emily," he told me. He was wearing the same Grateful Dead T-shirt he'd worn in my last dream. He looked awful. Worse than at the dance. And then he was gone.

I bolted upright and grabbed Brian's hand. "Get your car keys out!" I told him as I ran for the front door. "We're going into Boston! Now!"

Thirty minutes later, Carrie, Brian, and I drove through the Sumner Tunnel into downtown Boston. During every second of our ride, I thought about Jeremiah and my mother and my father. I felt awful about abandoning them, but the look in my brother's eyes had left me no choice. I had to get to him immediately. "Are you sure we shouldn't have called the police?" Carrie asked at least five times during the ride. She was sitting in the back seat, but she kept leaning forward over Brian's shoulder to make sure we heard her.

"Emily knows what she's doing," Brian told her, but I wasn't sure about that. "So where do you want me to go now?" he asked once we left the tunnel. "Should I head to the theater district? Or Washington Street? Or to the Common? Or Newbury Street? Cambridge? Boston College? Boston University?"

And then I knew. "To Kenmore Square. He's in a dorm at BU." I had no idea how I knew that, but it was as clear to me as the outline of Brian's adorable face as he removed his eyes from the road and turned to look at me. How had I ever been attracted to Jeremiah? The guy to my left was the best-looking, nicest, smartest guy I'd met in my entire life.

"Wow, Emmy," Carrie said from the back seat. "You're going to find Simon. You're just amazing."

"That she is," Brian agreed as he drove toward Storrow Drive. "But do you know which dorm, Emily? I know a few of them, but there are a lot of them on Bay State Road and Commonwealth Avenue."

I closed my eyes and tried to picture where my brother was. I'd never been to the BU campus. But it took only a second for me to see the twin towers connected by a small flat building. "The twin towers," I told Brian when I opened my eyes, and he nodded.

"I can't believe you, Emily!" Carrie gushed again. "You are the most incredible human being in the world."

"Didn't I tell you that all night?" Brian said, and I knew he had. And I knew she had agreed. I was deeply ashamed of the jealous feelings I'd had earlier. Carrie was my best friend. She loved me. And I loved her.

"Oh, God," Carrie said softly. "I just want to find Simon soon. I'm worried sick about him." And I leaned back to hug her. Poor Carrie. She really cared about Simon. I'd forgotten about that. Even though he'd barely paid any attention to her at the dance, she was nuts over him.

Carrie had no romantic feelings for Brian. But I did. And I was so lucky. I'd fallen for a great kid, but she was going after one of the world's toughest guys. Even if we found Simon right away and he was fine, he was never going to make her happy. He was Simon. He didn't make people happy. Then, in the middle of the hug, I saw Simon again. He was shaking his head back and forth at me. He looked terribly scared and completely different from the brother I'd seen all my life, and I had a strong sense that I was wrong about him. Maybe he could be decent. But of one thing I was certain. He was in trouble. And it was getting worse every second I was not beside him.

The minute Brian pulled his car onto Bay State Road, I knew I didn't have a second to spare. When Brian slowed the car down to wait for a space outside the twin towers dorm, I opened my door and raced out of the car. I looked up at the huge dorm, at least twenty floors tall, and knew what I had to do. Simon was on the top floor.

Ignoring Brian's and Carrie's pleas to wait for them, I lay down on the hard, cold sidewalk, shut my eyes, and concentrated with every bit of energy I could muster. *Get up there*, I told myself. *Get off this dumb sidewalk. Fly up there. Think of the fluffy white clouds and head for them. They're soft. They're delicious. You want to be there. Think about fish and water made out of glass. Go. Fly. Fly. Fly.* I concentrated so hard every muscle in my body ached. I could feel Carrie's hands on my stomach. I could feel Brian's hands on my shoulders. But I had no choice.

I had to get there. Immediately. Up, up, and away. For a brief second, I could feel the sidewalk begin to fall beneath me. I *was* getting up there. But then the cement hit my back with a resounding smack, and I opened my eyes. I was back on the sidewalk, a beached whale dying on the sand, and Brian and Carrie were standing over me, looking panicked.

I closed my eyes again. This was ridiculous. I'd done it before when it hadn't mattered. I could do it again. I just needed the right vision to propel me. It took a few seconds, but I got it. I thought of the day at my grandmother's lake when Simon had saved my life, and the next thing I knew I was airborne.

When my eyes opened, I was lying on the roof of the dormitory. I stood right up, opened the door on the roof, and walked into the building. I was on the top floor. Simon, I was positively certain, was in the room immediately to my right. The door to the room was unlocked, but I knocked anyhow. "Come in," a familiar voice said, and I did. My brother was in the room, handcuffed to a chair. And beside him, was the person with the familiar voice: Jeremiah.

fourteen
&

"*F*ancy meeting you here," Jeremiah greeted me. "I was hoping to avoid this but you're too fast for me." I couldn't speak. Jeremiah didn't look the least bit sexy to me. He just looked scary. "Say hi to your brother," he told me as I stood there, unable to speak or to move. "You did a great job finding him."

"Hi, there," Simon said when it was obvious no words were coming out of my mouth. "Do I know you from somewhere?"

"I'm your fat kid sister," I answered, and he smiled, and I was amazed I was able to speak and could make him smile. He was wearing his ragged Grateful Dead T-shirt, blue jeans, and sneakers. His hair was standing up all over his head, worse than his bum costume. I can't say he didn't still look handsome, but he looked worn out. His usual look of arrogance, the sneer that most females considered a captivating smile, was missing. My brother looked a lot worse than he did when he rolled into the house after a night of drinking.

His smile faded quickly. He looked . . . defeated. "What took you so long?" he asked me. "I thought you'd never get here."

"It took me a while to book the right flight," I told him, and he looked at me strangely.

"Don't tell me you're one of them," he asked me, and he looked, for the first time that I could remember, frightened. Then he covered his gross-looking hair with his hands. "And don't tell me you have wet broom tops and garlic. Every time I close my eyes, it's all I can see and smell."

I shook my head and refused to look at Jeremiah. I knew he was wearing the same cowboy shirt and black jeans he'd been wearing when he dropped my mother and me off at our house. "This is quite a room you have here," I said, talking to my brother as if Jeremiah were not in the room. All I saw in the room, besides the two guys, was an ugly brown couch with reddish stains and ripped pillows, a ratty-looking table with three unmatched and wobbly chairs, four red walls, and a soiled yellow rug. If this was the way college students lived, I'd rather stay home for four years.

"Gorgeous, huh?" Simon asked, as if he knew we shouldn't include Jeremiah in our conversation, and I smiled. Simon's room at home was handsomely decorated in black and white. There weren't too many good things I could say about my brother's behavior at home, but he was compulsively neat about his room. A couple of years before, in a rage over something he'd done, my mother had charged into Simon's room and emptied all his drawers onto the floor. When he walked into his room and saw what she had done, he'd come the closest to crying that I'd ever seen. You would have thought my mother would use that secret weapon against my brother again, but she never did.

Suddenly, just as I bent over to examine a poster

of a large, unidentifiable animal with wings and jag-
ged teeth on the wall behind Simon, Jeremiah grabbed
my arm. "Sit down," he ordered. I saw Simon flinch.
Jeremiah was hurting my arm, but I wasn't going to
let that creep make me cry. I was a strong, powerful
woman. I had just levitated to the roof of this dorm.
I could overcome that pathetic creature dressed in
black any time I wanted. Obviously, I didn't want to
do that just yet. "And don't move while I figure out
what I'm going to do with you."

I had no idea if Jeremiah knew that Brian and Carrie had driven me into Boston. I had no idea what he
was going to do with us, but from the evil look on
his face, I knew he wasn't going to serve us tea or
hold me securely on his lap. It didn't appear as if he'd
physically harmed my brother—not yet, anyhow. Jeremiah was a big bad dude, and I had been a very
stupid little girl.

"Why are you doing this, Jeremiah?" I asked, de-
ciding that my plan not to talk to him was not working
and trying to stall for time. "Is this all part of a magic
trick or a special witch ceremony?"

Jeremiah shoved me into a chair and pulled another
pair of handcuffs out of his back pocket. In a flash,
he had handcuffed my right hand to the back of the
chair. I had never felt so helpless, like a caged animal
about to be beaten. It took every bit of strength I could
muster not to begin to sob in front of my captor, but
I bit my tongue hard and mentally drew a shield
around my body. From the corner of my eye, I could
see the look on my brother's face, like he wanted to
kill Jeremiah. I sensed he was more afraid for me than
he was for himself. It didn't seem possible that my
brother could have such feelings for me. But it also
didn't seem possible that I had levitated twenty floors

to be handcuffed like a stupid weakling to a chair. "What's going on, Jeremiah?" I asked as demurely as I could. "This must be some kind of a joke, right? You're going to put on your cow costume any second, right?"

"Don't be an idiot," he answered sharply. He sat down in a chair beside me and ran his fingers through his hair. I had no desire to sit in his lap or run my fingers through his hair or look at his miserable face. But I kept working on my shield and drew a smile on my own face.

"None of this was supposed to work out this way," Jeremiah began, looking nervously from my brother to me to the strange animal poster beyond us. "I promised my mother I'd take care of your brother, and I meant to do that. Just get him out of the trouble he'd gotten himself into at the dance. And I did. I got him out of the school, the way she told me to. But then things went crazy."

I could tell I was talking to a disturbed person. Jeremiah waved his hands in front of his face as he talked, one minute animated and angry, the next still, his voice barely audible. There might not have been any black-and-blue marks on Simon's face or body, but my brother looked frightened enough to convince me he'd had some tough moments during the previous twenty-four hours. I knew I had to keep Jeremiah talking. Once he stopped, something terrible was going to happen. "So you didn't bring Simon to your mother's house?" I asked. "Or was Simon there while my mother and Brian and I were there this afternoon?"

"Of course he wasn't there," Jeremiah said, getting all worked up again, his face now red and angry. "Do you think I could get away with keeping him that close to my mother without her knowing?'' he continued, standing up. ''Hasn't she taught you anything? The woman is intuitive and powerful. The only reason I've been able to get away with as much as I have is because she's not well. She has a mild heart condition, which keeps her from using her full powers all the time. Strangely, my powers seem to get stronger when hers get weaker.''

''You really are amazing,'' I said as enthusiastically as I could. My hands were beginning to ache. I could imagine how Simon's must feel. ''I mean, your mother has taught me a few things, like how to levitate, but I could never be as good as you. And Simon has the same mother as you, but he sure can't do any of the things you can do.''

Unfortunately, that was not a good statement to make. ''Yeah, we sure do have the same mother,'' Jeremiah snarled. ''But you're wrong about his powers. Unfortunately, he has inherited some of hers. And what he's doing to her with them is disgusting. He might be my brother, but he's a pathetic character. He makes me sick. I spent my whole life wondering who and where my mother was, and when I finally found her and began to have a decent relationship with her, he comes along and ruins everything. She's been getting sick trying to straighten him out. She can't put out the kind of energy he needs.'' He banged his hand on my chair with such force that I hurt my own hand as I tried unsuccessfully to pull it toward my face. Simon looked every bit as nervous as I did. But Jeremiah did not hurt either one of us. Not yet, anyhow.

''She doesn't need this trouble from him,'' Jeremiah said, pacing as he spoke. I couldn't believe this was the same guy I'd seen in his mother's house or at my school. This Jeremiah was fierce and troubled.

How had he hidden that side from his mother, my mother, and me? Jeremiah Brooks was obviously a most talented witch.

"I never gave Sarah any trouble," he told me. "She was so proud of my grades and academic accomplishments. They were all she talked about until she found out about him. You should have seen how impressed she was when I sent in an application to Harvard two months ago, just for the fun of it, and got accepted there within four weeks." I had a fleeting thought of Jeremiah Brooks' application to Harvard. Had it included the fact that he was a warlock; could levitate and have out-of-body experiences; had two distinct personalities, one warm and gentle, the other a raging lunatic; and also knew how to destroy anyone who got between him and his long-lost mother?

"What are you smiling about?" Jeremiah asked, and I regretted allowing my mind to consider such an outrageous application. I hoped he wasn't able to read my mind.

"I was just thinking how brilliant you are," I said quickly. "Truthfully, you make Simon look so much worse by comparison. The closest he'll ever get to Harvard is attending one of its football games. You must be so wicked smart, Jeremiah."

His anger faded just a bit. "Yeah, well, I wasn't smart enough to convince your brother that he should go where I wanted him to go."

"And where was that?" I asked brightly. If Jeremiah wanted to pretend Simon wasn't in the room, that was fine. I'd play whatever game I had to play to get us out of there in one piece.

"To Seattle," Jeremiah answered. "I had the plane ticket for him. He—" He stopped talking and began looking strangely at my brother. I knew I had to keep him talking.

"That certainly was generous of you," I said. "I must tell you, Jeremiah, I just love that big car of yours. It's a BMW, isn't it? Is that car yours or is it Sarah's?" Guys were supposed to love their cars. I hoped Jeremiah was normal in that one respect.

He stopped staring at Simon and looked at me. "That's Sarah's car," he said calmly, the rage gone from his voice. "She makes a lot of money in her witch business, selling potions and doing readings for rich businessmen who won't make a financial move without checking it out with her. I know Sarah thinks I'm planning on studying medicine, but after living with her, I've decided to get a degree in business. Together, the two of us will be very, very rich." He stopped for just a second and then his eyes were back on Simon. "And there will be just two of us."

"What were you saying about the plane ticket?" I asked him, sensing I was losing this battle big-time.

Jeremiah glanced at me. For the moment, anyhow, I had him back. "I bought him a one-way, first-class ticket to Seattle. So he could meet his birth father. He would have liked Steve. Your parents would have understood he wanted to meet him."

I jumped right back in when Jeremiah stopped. "And Sarah liked this plan, too?"

"She didn't know about it," he told me. "I got him out of the dance and took him to the airport. It was my plan. And it would have worked. It was the perfect solution for all our problems. But would he take the ticket?" He glared at Simon with such hatred, I felt my body quiver.

"Oh, no," Jeremiah continued. His jaw tightened and his eyes looked even darker. "Moving to Seattle is not the path our brother wants to follow. But does he tell me that? No, he lies. Says sure, he'll go. Makes a big deal about saying good-bye to me at the airport, wishing me a good life and hoping we can get to know each other as brothers some time in the future. Then he goes into the airport, stays for about fifteen minutes, and comes back out and tries to hail a cab. Does he honestly think I would just drive off and leave him there? I waited, and when I saw him come out and try to get a cab, I grabbed him and brought him here. A kid who comes to Sarah to have his tarot cards read actually lives in this room, but he's out of town for a week. Lucky for us, huh?" I eked out a nod. Never had I felt so unlucky.

"Things would have been so much simpler if he'd just done what I told him to do," Jeremiah went on. "But now . . ."

I don't know what got into me, but I refused to think about Jeremiah and what was happening to me and Simon. Instead, I imagined a huge, beautiful fish leaping out of the water and covering me with a wave of pure, exquisitely colored water. The next thing I knew I was standing up and my handcuffs were off. I glanced at Simon, and I wasn't surprised to see that he, too, was standing up and that his handcuffs were lying, broken, at his feet. "Care to go for a ride?" my brother asked me, and he laughed, a laugh so loud it filled the entire room. I also wasn't surprised that the window was open, nor was I frightened when we jumped. Seconds later, we were both lying on the grass behind the dorm. Simon was the first to get to his feet. He grabbed my arm and helped me up. Nothing hurt. Except maybe my right ankle, just a tiny bit. "Are you okay?" Simon asked, hugging me.

"I'm great," I answered. "How about you?"

"My left ankle feels a little funny," he told me. "Let's get out of here." With our arms wrapped around each other, we limped toward the front of the building. Carrie and Brian were standing there, talking to two policemen. "We checked all over the building but we couldn't find her," Carrie was telling a tall, blond, good-looking policeman. "Please help us. I'm so worried!"

"What does this Emily look like?" the officer asked my two friends.

Simon was ready to limp over to the four of them, but I held him back. "Wait one second," I whispered. "I have to hear this."

Brian answered first. "She's beautiful." He pointed to Carrie. "She's about her height and weight. But she has dark brown eyes and dark brown hair and a heart-shaped face and dimples, and she's beautiful."

That did it. "Hey!" I cried out, and all four of the others gasped. Brian was the first to move. Instinctively, he seemed to know something was wrong with me as he gently drew my body close to his. Carrie made a beeline toward Simon and had just reached him when I glanced up. Something black was hurtling toward the ground behind where we were all standing.

"It's Jeremiah!" I shrieked. I tried to run toward the black object, but my foot hurt too much and Brian's arms were too tight to allow me to move. I stood there, nearly overcome with a searing pain, as the policemen took off in hot pursuit. Suddenly, everything went dark, but that was all right. I was back in the water with the brightly colored fishes, and my pain had vanished.

fifteen
♪

When I woke up, I was in my bed at home. I wasn't surprised to be there. Nor was there anywhere else I could think of that I would rather be. I had a fleeting image of a fast ride in a car and a visit to an emergency room, but it was all so vague. Maybe I'd dreamed it. My ankle was sore, and I remembered my jump, but when I reached down to touch my ankle, I felt an Ace bandage around it. The pain seemed a lot less than it had been right after the fall. My mother and father and Sarah were sitting in the room, staring at me. Suddenly, the questions began to race wildly through my mind. Who put the bandage on my ankle? How did I get from the sidewalk at BU to my bedroom? What happened to the policemen? What happened to Simon? To Jeremiah? Where were Carrie and Brian? And why was Sarah somewhere else than at 13 Derby Street?

"The policemen insisted on taking you to the emergency room near BU," Sarah told me. It didn't surprise me that she was back in my mind again. It was like she had a permanent key to the area. "Brian called your parents immediately, and they spoke to the doctor, who said both you and Simon had minor sprains but were fine otherwise. Brian drove you home. You barely woke up during the ride and have been sleeping ever since."

"It's about time she got up," my father grumbled. "She slept for almost twelve hours."

"She needed the sleep," my mother said. She was dressed, I noticed immediately, in a red sweater and blue jeans. "She's been through hell and back." I saw her glance at Sarah. It was not a loving look.

"She'll be fine now," Sarah said. I touched my arm. I—or "she"—was really there.

"I certainly hope she won't be handcuffed to any more chairs," my mother said.

That was it. I was back. "Could someone please tell me what else happened? I mean, how's Simon? And what happened to Jeremiah?"

There was a long silence while my mother glanced at Sarah, and Sarah glanced at my father, and he glanced at my mother, and she glanced back at Sarah. Then, I guess, Sarah got the nod. "Your brother is fine. He just went out for a bit to get some air. His ankle is a bit painful, too, though his injury doesn't seem to be as bad as yours. But yours will be okay. Jeremiah is no longer at the police station. He's at the hospital undergoing some tests."

"Did he hurt himself when he hit the ground?" I asked.

"Oh, no," Sarah said quite proudly. "He made a perfect landing. But we felt it was important that he be checked over."

"He's getting his head examined," my mother said bluntly. "The police insisted. Which you must agree is one terrific idea."

"The boy is off his rocker," my father added. The look Sarah gave him was a bit scary, considering she

156

was a pretty powerful witch. But my father doesn't scare easily. "They should put him in a locked room and throw away the key."

"He'll be out in no time," Sarah said, with that proud tone again.

"What's wrong with him?" I asked, hoping someone could answer that question for me.

Sarah was the first to try. "He allowed some feelings of jealousy to overwhelm his good sense," she told me. "It was a lot for him to learn about his mother and his brother and his powers in a relatively short period of time. You have to remember that he is a most unusual young man."

"You have to remember he was so desperate for his newly found mother to love him that he was willing to hurt anyone who stood in the way of his relationship with her," my mother added.

"He's one sick kid who should be put away forever," my father told us again, in case we'd forgotten.

"And is that what's really going to happen to him now?" I asked.

Sarah was first again. "Probably not. The police said they'll wait for the report from the psychiatrist. The handcuffs really weren't that strong, you know. I'm surprised you and Simon couldn't get out of them earlier. Jeremiah fed Simon plenty of pizza and Coke, and the trip to Seattle wouldn't have been so awful. Also, he did keep Simon out of big trouble at the dance. He never intended to hurt either of you."

"Oh, really?" my mother said sarcastically. "I suppose he never intended to throw my two kids out of the window."

"You saw that was no problem," Sarah pointed out. "Except for some slight ankle injuries, that would have been no big deal. Jeremiah never would have hurt his brother. Or Emily.''

''And he won't when they lock him up and throw away the key,'' my father informed her.

Sarah looked ready to send my father on an out-of-body experience somewhere very far away. My mother must have sensed the danger. ''We probably won't press charges if he promises to get plenty of help,'' she said.

My father looked ready to tell us about the key situation again, but Simon, Carrie, and Brian saved him from his OBE to another planet. ''Hey, you're finally up,'' Simon greeted me, handing me a heavy, brightly wrapped package. My brother looked terrific, as handsome and well-groomed as ever and with a smile I'd rarely seen on his face. ''Here's a little something for my daring rescuer.''

''We all helped pick it out,'' Carrie said, kissing me on the top of the head. ''And your parents paid for it.''

''Hey, I pitched in a bit,'' Simon said, smiling at her. She smiled back. ''I used the money I planned to buy you a tofu burger with tonight.''

''Well, I'll just have to buy *you* a tofu burger,'' she told him. I couldn't believe it. Simon didn't eat tofu, and he was never in a room with me for more than five minutes without insulting me. Plus, never ever did he buy me a present. Maybe I was dreaming. Maybe I really wasn't there.

''You're going to love it,'' Brian said as he leaned over and, right in front of everyone, kissed me gently on my cheek. I was definitely there.

After I caught my breath, I took my time opening the package. Simon had his hand on one of Carrie's shoulders, but his eyes were on my face. Slowly, I pulled a luxuriously soft, black cape from the box. "It's cashmere," my brother informed me as he let go of Carrie and wrapped the cape around my shoulders. "It'll make your next flight a little easier."

I saw the looks on my parents' faces. They were sickeningly happy. And then I looked at Sarah. There was no look of joy on her face. As if she could tell I was looking at her, she stood up. "I think I'll take off now," she said, looking only at me. "As long as you're feeling all right, there's no reason for me to stay."

"Sure thing," my father said. "See you later."

" 'Bye," Simon said, barely glancing at her. "Take care."

"You, too," she said. "And please come by any time you want."

"Thanks," Simon said, but she didn't have to be a witch to understand that he probably wouldn't.

I wasn't surprised when my mother followed Sarah out of my room. "It's her herbal healing business," my father informed us when the two women were gone. "She's nuts about the effects and powers of herbs now. Forget about her writing career. Sarah's going to help her get started selling herbs."

"But they hate each other," I said.

"You've lost your intuitive senses," my father said. "Your mother was just acting like that for my benefit. She and Sarah are going to be good friends and possibly even business partners. I can't stand the woman, but I do admit she's a shrewd businesswoman. Mark my words. She and your mother are going to make a lot of money. Who knows? I may even give up my hardware store and retire. Stranger things have happened."

"Speaking of stranger things," my brother said to me, "are you up to a little drive?"

I knew exactly where he wanted to go, and I wanted to go, too. It was good to know that some of my new powers were still with me. My ankle didn't hurt much when I put my foot down on my bedroom rug, and my father didn't object when I got dressed in the bathroom, arranged the cape firmly around my body, and headed for Simon's car. Carrie and Brian came along for the ride, but it was clear before we got to the hospital that just Simon and I would speak to Jeremiah.

Jeremiah was sitting by himself in a small waiting room, reading, when Simon and I found him. He was wearing jeans and a maroon-and-white Harvard sweatshirt. He looked completely embarrassed when he saw the two of us. "Hi," he greeted us shyly. I could not remember Jeremiah's ever being shy or blushing the way he was now.

"How you doing?" Simon asked, pulling up a chair beside Jeremiah.

"Okay," Jeremiah said. "How about you two?"

"We're fine," Simon said. "Just a couple of sore ankles from our mighty flights. I was dying to tell the doctor at the emergency room exactly how we hurt our ankles, but I felt it was better not to go into the whole story."

"They had a hard enough time with my story," Jeremiah said, smiling a little now. He had not yet glanced at me, but that was okay. I was having a hard enough time being in the same room with him, never mind talking to him. He was still great-looking, but that wasn't it. I didn't feel attracted to him. All I felt was sad. Really sad.

I listened to the conversation between Jeremiah and

Simon and understood it was important I add nothing to it. "I don't want to get to know Sarah that much more," Simon told Jeremiah bluntly. "You don't have to worry about my getting in the way of your relationship with her. I have my own mother. I don't need another one."

"Sarah's an amazing lady," Jeremiah told Simon. "You should give her a chance."

"I'm sure that's true," Simon said. "But I have enough trouble getting along with one mother."

"She's going to want to get to know you," Jeremiah told him.

"That's fine," Simon said. "She can get to know me if she wants. But I think I know enough about her to take care of my interest."

"Are you interested in meeting Steve?" Jeremiah asked him.

"Not at all," Simon answered. "Like I told you before, one mother and one father is more than enough for me."

"I might go back to Seattle for a while when I get out of here," Jeremiah told him.

"That sounds like a good idea," Simon said, and I got a funny feeling. Not like I would miss him, but that both my life and Simon's would be different without him around.

"Don't you want to get to know more about your powers?" Jeremiah asked him.

"Not really," Simon said. "I'm not so sure I want to depend on them. I think they could be a real problem if I focused on them too much."

"But it's who you are, man," Jeremiah said. He was getting a bit upset and I was getting a bit nervous.

"No, it's not," Simon said. "It's just something extra I can do that others can't."

"Sarah has some great books you might want to read," Jeremiah said. He was calm again now. "I found them fascinating. Can I show you a few?"

"Sure," Simon said. "But, like I said, it's not that big a deal to me."

"Do you ski?" Jeremiah asked.

"Yeah," Simon said.

"Maybe we can ski together this winter," Jeremiah suggested. "I can teach you some tricks on the mountain, if you'd like." When Simon laughed, Jeremiah began to talk about his experiences at Vail and Heavenly Valley, and the conversation seemed perfectly normal. Like two guys enjoying each other's company. Maybe even like two brothers getting to know one another.

When Simon and Jeremiah finished talking about their ski experiences and the emergency room and the policemen at BU, they both glanced at me. "Neat cape," Jeremiah told me. "How's your ankle?"

"Just a little sore," I said.

"I'm really sorry about what happened," Jeremiah said. "I don't know what got into me. I don't know who that person was in that red room. But I guess that's why I'm here. To figure out who he was and to make sure he doesn't show up again."

Simon stood up and walked over to the window. I wasn't sure if he was giving me time alone with Jeremiah or if he was uncomfortable and needed a few minutes to gather his thoughts. "I've never seen you so quiet," Jeremiah finally said to me. "I know you're still frightened of me. I wish there was something I could say to make you feel better about me. I wish there was something I could say to make *me* feel better about me."

He looked so sad and uncomfortable, I couldn't

bear it. I stood up and walked over to where he sat. "I'm not frightened of you," I said, and I meant it. There was so much I wanted to tell Jeremiah. How scared I was about magic that let me levitate twenty floors or leap out a window or make doors open or turn klutzy soccer players into stars. But when Jeremiah reached out and held my hand, it didn't seem necessary to tell him what I was frightened about. I knew he understood. And that made most of the fear go away.

When I left Jeremiah's room, I was still very worried about him. I didn't need to be a psychiatrist to know that he had serious problems to work out and that all the magic in the world wasn't going to make that an easy job. I was pleased, however, that my brother stayed with Jeremiah. I saw the way Simon looked at Jeremiah. He wasn't afraid of him at all. And Jeremiah had to understand that. They were, after all, brothers, sons of the same witch.

Brian and Carrie and I sat in the main waiting room of the hospital for nearly an hour waiting for Simon. We talked about what had happened at BU and what would probably happen to Jeremiah. "He's not normal," Carrie said. "But he sure is gorgeous."

"I think he's going to need a lot of help," Brian said as he sat beside me on the couch, holding my hand. "We'll never know what he planned to do to you and Simon if you hadn't escaped."

"Simon talked to me about that," Carrie told us. "He believes that Jeremiah had no idea what he was going to do. He's convinced that Jeremiah knew you two could break out of the handcuffs if you really tried and he helped you do that. What do *you* think would have happened, Emmy?"

I closed my eyes for a few minutes before answering. And then it became perfectly clear to me. "I think Sarah finally broke through Jeremiah's powers and got herself into that room," I said, my eyes wide open now. "I think she was the one who helped us break out of the handcuffs. Once she finally got into the act, everything happened exactly the way she wanted. Jeremiah's getting the help she couldn't give him, and Simon and Jeremiah just might begin to form some sort of a relationship that may allow them to become brothers."

"Wow," Brian said. "What a thought. But what about you? What did she want from you?"

"Probably to be there for Jeremiah," Carrie answered, and I nodded.

Brian looked so worried that I leaned over and kissed him. "But Sarah doesn't always get her wish," I told him. Suddenly, I felt a weird shiver flow through my body. But, as quickly as it had come, it passed. I understood at that exact moment that my soccer star days might well be over. And I might not be able to open any lockers without the combinations. Or touch the ceiling of my bedroom. But the way Brian squeezed my hand told me that I didn't need a witch to make me feel pretty special about myself.

In the Enchanted Hearts *series, romance with just a touch of magic makes for love stories that are a little more perfect than real life.*

In Cherie Bennett's Love Him Forever, *the sixth title in the series, Colleen undergoes hypnosis in order to experience past life regressions for an article in the school paper. She finds out more than she bargained for, though, and soon is faced with a choice between her steady boyfriend Kevin and mysterious new-in-town Luke, both of whom are present in each of her past lives.*

Love Him Forever

Ø

*P*assionate. *That was how Colleen Belmont thought of* herself. Passionate was definitely good.

Tempestuous. That was how Tolliver Heath thought of her. He also thought she was volatile, unreasonable, and melodramatic. All of which were definitely bad.

As Tolliver pontificated to the staff of the *Lakesider*, the oh-so-imaginatively-named student newspaper of Lakeside High School, Colleen raised her index finger into the air. She knew Tolliver was watching her, because he was always watching her. The editor in chief had the world's hugest crush on Colleen, and everyone knew it.

He stopped mid-sentence. "Yes, Colleen?"

She smiled at him sweetly. Her loathing for him didn't show a bit. "Well, Tollie," she began, "remember our discussion at last week's editorial meeting about my proposed new paranormal phenomena column for the paper?"

"Yes, what of it?" Tollie resettled his glasses on his skinny nose. He was tall and so thin that his expensive clothes hung on his body as if it were a coat rack. No one had ever seen him in jeans. The entire newspaper staff had an ongoing betting pool—a confirmed sighting of Tollie in jeans was worth fifty bucks.

So far, no one had come close to collecting.

Tolliver, or Tollie, as he insisted he be called, ran editorial meetings of the school paper like they were Strategic Air Command crisis strategy sessions for global thermonuclear war. Colleen was sure he had never cracked a joke in his entire life. And she seriously doubted he had actual bodily functions.

"Well, Tollie," Colleen went on sweetly, "I've taken the liberty of writing up a few samples of the column—I'm thinking of calling it 'Beyond Reason'— and I thought we could try one out in next week's issue of the paper." She got up and handed a few sheets of paper to Tolliver.

"That's a great idea!" Betsy Wu exclaimed. She was Colleen's best friend and the newspaper's sports reporter. "This school could stand a little excitement. I vote we give it a try."

Tolliver gave Betsy a contemptuous look. "Might I point out that you haven't even read the samples yet."

"They're Colleen's," Betsy said with a shrug. "She's the best writer on the paper, so they must be great."

"And here I thought Celeste was the best writer on this paper," Brandon Marrow joked. He was a junior who covered music and dance.

"Please don't mention the Curls," Betsy said. "She's out sick, and I for one am thrilled with the reprieve."

"Might we stick to the subject at hand, people?" Tolliver asked.

"We might, Tollie, my man," Kevin Armour replied. "Colleen's idea is great. I say we go for it."

Colleen smiled radiantly in Kevin's direction.

Big mistake. Tollie's nostrils twitched. That was never good.

You know you can never, ever show attention to any other guy in front of Tolliver, Colleen admonished herself, *even if Tollie knows you are going out with the guy to whom you're showing attention, because Tolliver's maggot-size ego can't take the comp.*

And she wouldn't have slipped up if it hadn't been for the fact that she knew Kevin actually detested her paranormal column idea. She'd just been completely surprised when he'd publicly supported it anyway.

Colleen and Kevin had been a couple for almost a year. Kevin's parents were both involved in the theater, and they had moved to Milwaukee from their home in New York City to do a year-long residency at the University of Wisconsin's Milwaukee campus and to work at Milwaukee Repertory Theatre. Kevin was much more interested in photography—he was the number-one news photographer for the *Lakesider*.

Even Betsy, who had been brutal on all of Colleen's previous boyfriends (of whom there had been exactly three since seventh grade), thought they made a great couple. Lots of people said Kevin resembled the tennis player Peter Sampras. He had Sampras's thick, curly, dark hair; electric, dark eyes; and easy, open grin. He habitually had a camera, and sometimes two, around his neck, and was forever telling Colleen that what he cared about was what *was*, not what *might be*. That was woo-woo stuff, as he called it. He was the ultimate skeptic.

Colleen, on the other hand, was, if not the ultimate believer, at least the ultimate in open-mindedness. Her Ouija board had been her favorite Christmas gift when she was ten, and she used the same board now to commune with what she called "Other Worlds."

She had the classic petite Irish good looks of her mother, who had come to the United States from Dublin as a little girl. Her bright-red, wavy hair was her trademark—it reached down nearly to the bottom of her back. Her skin was pale and beautiful, her eyes were an intense shade of blue, and she was famous for the antique pins she collected from garage sales and thrift shops.

Colleen loved to write, especially about movies. Her goal was to replace Roger Ebert as the movie critic at the *Chicago Sun-Times*. She was pretty confident she could do it, too.

So was everyone else.

What she wasn't confident about was whether or not she could get through high school without strangling Tolliver Heath's scrawny chicken-skinned neck. He was utterly, royally, dictatorial and unfair. She *hated* that.

Tolliver sighed. "Colleen, this is a school newspaper, not a tabloid supermarket scandal sheet full of made-up supernatural garbage."

"My column would not be supernatural garbage, as you so eloquently put it, Tollie," Colleen retorted. She could feel herself getting angrier, the color rising to her cheeks.

Chill, she told herself. *You've worked so hard to keep your temper in check lately. You can do it, you can do it, you can do it. You know you can do it.*

"There's more and more research being done in this area, and important discoveries are being made almost every day," she said, keeping her voice even. "All I'm asking is that you look at my sample articles, Tollie. Please?"

"Come on, Tol," Kevin urged him. "You know Colleen rocks, so give her a break."

Bad move. Tollie's nostrils quivered like Jell-O in an earthquake.

"I would have to have rocks in my head to approve this swill," Tollie replied, shuffling through Colleen's articles. " 'Ouija and Your SATs'? 'How to Change Your Aura in Sixty Seconds'? 'Past Life Regression for High School Students in Five Easy Steps'?" He threw the articles onto the desk. "May I vomit now, or shall I wait until later?"

Colleen's face grew redder. "It so happens I asked my Ouija board what the big essay question was going to be on our history final last marking period. And I seem to recall I aced that test—"

"Unlike someone we know," Betsy put in, and pushed a strand of blood-red hair out of her face. Very petite, with a round face and beautiful almond-shaped eyes, her alternative style was legendary. At the moment she wore a long bottle-green plaid skirt with an oversized orange-and-red sweater, one of her more conservative looks. She'd added a streak of red and a streak of green to her hair, in honor of its being close to Christmas.

Tolliver shot Betsy a dirty look. He'd gotten a B in history last marking period, the very first B of his life. If that wasn't bad enough, everyone had made buzzing noises around him for more than a week afterward. He'd been so depressed that it had taken days for him to realize they were buzzing like a bee. Haha.

"That B was a tiny stitch in the fabric of my life," Tolliver huffed. "The fact remains that these—*your*—so-called columns are not fit to run in my newspaper.

Not now, not tomorrow, and not forever, not in any paper of which I am in charge.''

''But—'' Colleen began.

Tolliver ignored her. ''Now, since we are, by my calculations, two minutes behind, we'll move on to the next order of business, the publicity for our College Bowl team. The team will be—''

''You're not even going to take them home to read them through?'' Colleen asked.

''I prioritize, Colleen,'' Tollie informed her. ''Jokes such as your column make my list somewhere under 'Extra Time Spent Dental Flossing.' Now, where was I? Ah, yes. The College Bowl team is—''

''—about as interesting as the last editorial you wrote,'' Colleen broke in. Her cheeks were flaming now, but she didn't care. ''I mean, please, Tolliver, you think we should return to the dress code of the nineteen-fifties? No one in the entire school but you owns the wardrobe for it!''

''This is great,'' Brandon muttered gleefully. The entire staff was watching, grins on their faces. They never interrupted a good fight between Tollie and Colleen. It was always the best part of an editorial meeting. A couple of them even formed their hands into the shape of guns and blew imaginary smoke away from the tips of their index fingers.

Yikes, Betsy thought. *Bad move, Colleen. Criticize anything you want about Tolliver, but don't criticize his editorials.*

''Although it was an interesting point of view,'' Betsy called to Tollie, hoping to rescue her friend.

Tollie never even heard her. He glared at Colleen. ''Let me remind you my editorial was submitted by the administration to the National Board of Student

Newspapers for the Best Editorial of the Year Award.''

"Big duh, Tollie," Colleen replied. "Our principal went to high school in the fifties, which is the last time he had anything resembling a life. That was a suck-up editorial and you know it, Tolliver. You just want that award for your application to Yale."

Kevin groaned and slumped in his seat. Betsy shook her head sadly. They'd both seen Colleen's mouth get the better of her too many times. She could never stand by silently when someone was treating someone else unfairly. Especially if the someone was her.

Tolliver leaned over the table toward Colleen. She could see the little hairs inside his quivering nostrils. It wasn't pretty. "I am staying calm because I am a professional," he told her. "Now, for the last time, no insipid occult column. We only print stories of real interest to our peers. And that's final!"

"Cool," Betsy agreed, hoping to end the conversation. "So, moving on to that swell College Bowl thingie—"

Colleen stood up and leaned toward Tolliver. "You don't think our peers care more about the paranormal than they did about your weenie editorial?" she challenged. "What was it that happened the day after your brilliant editorial ran? Right, now I remember. Everyone came to school dressed in Tolliver Heath–approved bow ties."

"And they weren't so easy to find, Tollie, I gotta tell you," Brandon pointed out. "I looked all over Milwauk—"

Tolliver slammed his palm on the table. Colleen jumped. His eyes grew cold. They bore into hers. "Don't push me, Colleen."

For just a moment, she thought he looked scary. Like, really, *really* scary. But that was just her vivid imagination. This was Tolliver Heath, she reminded herself, not the hook guy from *I Still Know What You Did Last Summer.*

"And don't you push me, Tollie," Colleen replied. "I'm not going to pretend that you're making this decision in the best interests of the paper. Because you're not."

"As editor in chief, I—"

"Here's three chords and the truth, Tollie," Colleen interrupted. "You're not going to win this time."

The room was so quiet they could all hear the cheerleaders practicing in the gym at the other end of the school. Tolliver composed himself. He hated being out of control. And he didn't dare to push Colleen off the newspaper. For one thing, she was the best writer he had. And for another . . .

Well. That was private.

"I'll overlook your behavior this time," Tolliver said, pushing at his glasses. "Now, we have—"

"Wow, look at the time." Colleen grabbed her backpack and headed for the door. "I almost forgot, the new Spielberg movie's opening at the Cinema Center today."

"But what about the rest of the meet—"

"Sorry, Tollie, guess I've got to go review it. You wouldn't want me to have an empty space where my movie column would be, would you? Or would you rather we just pop in one of those occult articles? I didn't think so."

Tolliver stood there, helpless, as she walked out of the newspaper office and clicked the door closed behind her. There was really nothing he could say. After all, she *was* the paper's movie critic, and the new movie *was* opening. She was merely doing her job. He sat down and shuffled his papers. He was way past quivering nostrils. Now his hands shook, and his jaw was clenched so tightly the veins stood out in his neck.

Betsy leaned toward Kevin. "Score: Belmont, one; Heath, goose egg."

"Never get cocky about the score in the second inning, I always say," Kevin replied. Lately something about Heath had been giving him the creeps. "If I know Tollie, he's going to try to get back at her. Soon."

Colleen was lost in thought at her computer. She'd been writing, but her mind had begun to wander. When she left the newspaper meeting that afternoon, she'd almost run headlong into Luke Ransom. He was new, a senior who had moved to Lakeside from New Orleans. His eyes were light blue, his chin chiseled, his body lanky, his walk sinewy. Colleen had never even spoken to him. But sometimes she would feel this heat, and she'd turn around, and those blue, blue eyes would be staring at her, through her, seeing everything.

Yeah, right. She shook off the feeling. Her vivid imagination was just getting the best of her, that was all. So the guy was hot. Lots of guys were hot. She was in love with Kevin.

She forced herself to concentrate on her writing, and began typing again. Someone knocked on her door.

"Go away," she called out, and kept typing.

"Aren't you even going to ask who it is?" her little sister, Kat, demanded through the door.

"I know who it is," Colleen replied.

"Can I come in?"

"No. I'm working."

"On what?"

"On none of your business."

"What's none of my business?" Kat called back.

Colleen groaned and began counting down from the number ten silently. *She's going to be through that door by the time I reach six,* she thought to herself. *Ten, nine, eight—*

The door popped open, and Kat stuck her head in. Her dark ponytail poked through the back of her baseball cap, and she wore a red, white, and blue Davis Cup–style warm-up suit. Only eleven, Kat was a ranked tennis player not only in her own age group in the state of Wisconsin but also in the under-14 category.

"Well, what a surprise to have you just walk in after I asked you nicely to go away," Colleen said.

Kat plopped down on Colleen's bed and bounced up and down. "You didn't ask nicely. You asked meanly."

"It's really too bad your maturity on the court doesn't extend to the rest of your life," Colleen said. "Stop bouncing."

Kat stopped by popping up from the bed onto her feet. She went to peer over her sister's shoulder at the computer screen. Colleen quickly hit a key to black it out.

"No fair!" Kat cried. "What were you writing, porno?"

Colleen gave her a withering look.

Kat shrugged. "Okay, be like that. I only came up here to tell you that tall, dark, and dorky is downstairs."

This was Kat's usual description of Kevin, whom

she actually thought was so cute she could hardly breathe around him.

"Why didn't you say so?" Colleen asked, quickly backing up what she'd just written.

"I just did. Hey, can I hang out with you guys?" Kat bent over and ostentatiously began stretching out her hamstrings. "That is, after I give you five minutes for spit swapping and stuff."

Colleen got up. "No, you cannot hang out with us."

"Why not?"

"Because I said so. Kevin came over to read something that I wrote."

"Can I read it, too?"

"No." Colleen headed for the stairs. "Go study. When Mom and Dad get home, they'll want to check your math."

"I hate math. It's stupid." She hung over the banister and called down to Colleen. "What does a professional tennis player need with math, anyway, except to count money?"

Colleen ignored her and went into the living room, where Kevin was looking through one of Kat's tennis magazines.

He is so cute, she thought. He looked up and gave her a heart-melting grin.

"Hi," he said softly. "How was the movie?"

She sat next to him on the couch "What movie?" she asked. "I thought we could see it together this weekend. I just said that to get Tolliver's undies in a wad. Boxers, not briefs, I'm sure."

Kevin laughed. "Well, it worked. You were brilliant at the meeting. I mean, it was futile, empty, and senseless. But you won."

"I know I shouldn't fight with him," Colleen admitted.

"True."

"It's counterproductive to my goals."

Kevin nodded. "Also true."

"But I just—"

As Colleen said "can't help myself," Kevin said "can't help yourself," and they both laughed. She leaned over and kissed his cheek softly.

He reached for her, then stopped. "Is Kat still upstairs?"

"I told her to do math."

"Parents?"

"Out."

"Good." His steely dark eyes searched hers. The first time he had done that, when they'd first kissed back in February, she'd felt an electric rush through her entire body. His heat had melted her. And then his kisses made her burst into flames.

They still did.

His lips met hers. Softly at first, then more insistently. Eyes closed, she lost herself in the bliss of his kisses.

Oh, Luke . . .

Colleen gasped and opened her eyes. Thank God she hadn't said aloud what she'd been thinking. Kevin would never, ever forgive her if she moaned out another guy's name when he was kissing her. She loved Kevin. And she loved his kisses. So why was she thinking about—

"Hey, are you okay?" Kevin asked.

"Fine," she assured him. "Where were we?"

"Oh, about here." He brought his lips to the pulse in her throat and kissed her so softly, she shivered. "Hey, I want to talk about your birthday."

"And I want you to do that again, only on my lips," Colleen said, reaching for him.

He smiled. "It's in a month, right?"

"January first, same as last year, thirty days from today." She leaned forward and began to kiss him again.

He kissed her lightly. "How about a birthday brunch at the Adams Mark? That is, after we spend New Year's Eve together."

"Sure, sounds great. More kissing."

From the top of the stairs, Kat peered down. The hallway was empty. Good. That meant her sister was probably sucking face with tall, dark, and dorky in the living room. Which was just the opportunity Kat needed.

She darted into Colleen's room and hit the enter key on the computer so that the screen would come up again. Anytime her sister told her she couldn't do something, it made her want to do it even more. Colleen had certainly not wanted Kat to see what she was writing. Well, Kat was about to see it, anyway.

The screen filled. Kat read it quickly.

And then she screamed.

Phyllis Karas is the author of *Cry Baby* and *The Hate Crime* from Avon Flare and *For Lucky's Sake* from Avon Camelot.

She teaches at the Boston University School of Journalism and writes for *People* magazine. She lives with her family in Marblehead, Massachusetts.

A fantasy, a love story, a summer of change...

The China Garden

By LIZ BERRY

AVON
tempest

"Like a jewel box with hidden drawers and compartments, this finely crafted, multilayered novel holds many secrets...richly laden with mystery and suspense, in which the ordinary often masks unexpected interconnections and the extraordinary is natural to the story's wildly imagined terrain."
—PUBLISHERS WEEKLY ☆

Love stories just a little more perfect than real life...

Don't miss any in the
enchanted ♥ HEARTS
series:

ehs 0499

Nothing in my life was normal anymore. I wasn't normal anymore. I had a mad crush on Brian. Brian had invited me to the dance. I thought Jeremiah was absolutely gorgeous. Jeremiah had come to my school to see me. I quickly glanced at my locker, remembered the combination, and the door immediately swung open without my touching the lock. Yup, this was my life now. "Hi, Jeremiah," I said, smiling broadly. "What's up?"

"I thought I'd drive you over to the hardware store," he said.

"Great idea," I said, noticing that Jeremiah's eyes were so black they gave *black* a new meaning. *Black* now meant shimmering and sexy and luminous and powerful and red-hot. Brian Walsh might have been cute, but this figure standing in front of my locker was sumptuous.